Water Runs
Slow Through
Flat Land

CLIFF JONES

Cover illustration by Lucy Pepper
www.lucypepper.com

ISBN 10: 1507852568
ISBN-13: 978-1507852569

To my family – for their support and love, and for never letting me forget that life is what's right in front of you.

1
Tuesday 17 August 2010
Afghanistan

The dusty, rippled landscape surrounding Kabul rose to meet him like a slow tide as the ageing Boeing lurched towards the airport, two and a half hours and a world away from Dubai's hotels and shopping malls.

Peter grabbed the napkins offered to him by the flight attendant.

"I am so sorry," she said. "I dropped one can before, but I thought this was a different one."

He handed her back the can of Ginger Ale and held the plastic cup of Jack Daniel's.

"Fine, it's fine," said Peter, irritated, tilting his tray towards the seat back in front of him. "Most of it went on the tray."

The pale liquid fizzed on the table tray top and trickled down onto the thin carpet by his feet. His shoes made a sticking noise as he moved them on the floor.

The flight attendant excused herself and reappeared with a damp cloth and cleaned the table. She looked at Peter's shirt, speckled by the mist of soda. "I apologise, please. You will forgive me."

"Don't worry about it," said Peter. "Can I have another cloth please?"

"Of course." The woman said something in Pashto to the purser who had come to investigate the commotion. He responded and walked back to the galley.

"Can I get you anything else? Another drink?"

"No thank you. At least the whiskey survived."

Her colleague returned with more napkins. Peter took them and carefully wiped around the plastic cup that held the bourbon. "I'll have it neat," he said.

He put the cup back down on the tray. The flight attendant watched him with concern.

The purser looked at his colleague accusingly before turning to Peter. "If you need anything," he said, "please ask."

Peter nodded and turned to the window. He looked at the city below him and the mountains beyond. He didn't want to answer, but it wasn't to spare the flight attendant any further embarrassment, it was to save his own. He hated small talk and was uncomfortable in conversation with people he didn't know. He knew these weren't the best attributes for a journalist.

How he expressed himself often landed him in the furthest reaches of trouble, sometimes as far as tarnishing the name even of anyone who tried to stand up for him.

He could hold water only slightly better than a secret because he found facts more appealing than discretion. He couldn't resist telling the truth even if it was hurtful and especially if it got a laugh.

Peter could incriminate himself online by not thinking before he typed. He had worked for NPL since shortly after it launched, and he headed up the team in the early days of internet newsrooms. Twitter and Facebook were still some years down the line when he joined, and their arrival provided the platform for Peter to put a foot wrong so badly it was like a man running into a dark room full of rakes.

2
Friday 25 June 2010
Ealing, London

Peter was watching the BBC's Glastonbury coverage in his one bedroom Ealing flat while the rain outside soaked the western reaches of London. The presenters in the backstage TV studio introduced Snoop Dogg and warned the viewers that there could be swearing. Snoop didn't disappoint when inside of a minute he said "motherfuckers".

Peter knew there was a joke in there somewhere and he launched the Twitter app on his BlackBerry before he even knew what he was going to say.

He composed an update in his head.

OMG. The man on the BBC just said motherfuckers. I for one am shocked.

He thought twice about typing it in and hitting the Send button to put it live. He was a journalist approaching forty, in the respectable position of editor of the world's largest online news service and he was concerned that people would expect him to know better than to even mention a reference to a deplorable word.

He decided against it. Too many people from work followed him on Twitter and read his updates. However amusing it was to Peter that the BBC had just broadcast the word, he couldn't bring himself to use it.

But he wondered who would.

He typed the words "motherfuckers Glastonbury" into the box and clicked the button marked Search. A message appeared.

No Tweet results for motherfuckers, Glastonbury

He typed an update into the box marked *What's happening?* and updated his status.

Strong words from the BBC there.

He hit Send, the page reloaded, and his words were published above the message *Status updated.* He thought it was a disappointing update, a tweet half hatched by his standards, out of context and not very funny.

The concert went on, and so did the bad language, but the broadcast stayed on the air. Peter took dark amusement in considering the complaints the BBC would almost certainly receive. He pictured the Controller of BBC 2 shuffling in their seat at home.

He wondered how quickly complaints about swearing were sent in during live programmes. He believed complaining to the BBC about swearing was an ingrained behaviour among some viewers who saw the corporation as the last outpost of decency in a land they imagined to be without expletives.

He wanted to know if anyone had been offended right then, while Snoop was still on the stage. He typed another search into the box.

BBC motherfuckers

He clicked the button. The page reloaded and the message appeared under the window.

Status updated.

Then he looked at the Search button. The blood drained from his face as he saw the timeline next to his picture and he read his latest update.

"Oh my dizzy Christ," he said.

His mouth dried as his mind raced through a list of everyone who would read the two word entry. *What's happening?* read the question in front of the status update box. He had clicked the wrong button, mistakenly broadcasting a search query as a status update. What was happening, according to Peter at least, was *BBC motherfuckers*.

It took the summer's longest minute to delete, but the damage had been done. He removed the update in haste and shame but he knew it would have appeared on the screens of at least fifty people, a conservative estimate based on the seventeen thousand people who followed his updates. It was pointless to speculate who they might be, and he thought about how he could limit the damage.

He knew a strong retraction would only draw attention to a message he hoped no one had seen. He considered blaming a hacker but his defence wouldn't stand up to scrutiny, since the message would be tagged as having been sent from his BlackBerry.

Peter was aware that none of his followers would use Twitter to reply to the message to give him a chance to explain. Those who had seen it would be as shocked as he was, but for different reasons.

3
Sunday 27 June 2010
Ealing

Peter was relieved that no one had retweeted the message to share the joke or spread the outrage, and for a time he assumed that no apparent damage had been done, at least until that evening when he checked his messages on his phone in bed, as he did every night. He saw an email from Jim Edwards, his deputy on the newsdesk.

Date: 27 June, 2010. 10:26:05 GMT+1
From: Jim.Edwards@corp.npl.com
To: Jamie.Barbour@corp.npl.com,
Luci.Barlow@corp.npl.com, Sarah.Copland@corp.npl.com,
Mark.Lambeth@corp.npl.com, Carla.Abbot@corp.npl.com,
Richard.Garrett@corp.npl.com;
Cc: Peter.Beckenham@corp.npl.com
Subject: Tweet from @PBeckenham
Message:

BBC motherfuckers
http://twitter.com/#!/PBeckenham/status/12156479580

-Anyone else see this? Do you think the pressure has finally got to him? ;)
Jim

The names on the forwarded email were friendly colleagues who could take a joke, but the accidental Twitter update was being emailed, and even if people hadn't seen it on Twitter, a record of it had been sent to people he worked with.

Peter replied, to Jim only.

Date: 27 June, 2010. 19:51:18 GMT+1
From: Peter.Beckenham@corp.npl.com
To: Jim.Edwards@corp.npl.com
Subject: Re: Tweet from @PBeckenham
Message:

Talk tomorrow.

4
Monday 28 June 2010
Hammersmith, London

The morning brought with it a damp sky like lead, soft and heavy. Sarah Copland had been checking for Peter's updates, waiting to see how her colleague would follow his mistake. She held her phone to her chest to shelter it from the thin, light rain which had started to fall as she left her flat in Gloucester Road.

She and Peter would have lunch together once or twice a month, usually with colleagues, but sometimes on their own, although they had never met alone outside of the office. They enjoyed each other's company and they joked and flirted. Sarah thought little of the talk and held no expectations of consequences, although she knew Peter had divorced within eighteen months of a marriage in his early thirties. She was wary, knowing his whip-smart repartee would drive a lover away but this did little to smother her attraction to him, which she thought could be mutual. She checked her Twitter feed one last time before heading into the tube station.

She saw Jim on the station platform at Earl's Court and moved close enough to where he was standing so as not to seem unfriendly. She stood just outside the proximity of an unavoidable conversation but close enough to board the same carriage when the train arrived. The position was more for his comfort than hers. Sarah could talk easily with anyone, but she knew Jim Edwards was a shy, though friendly man, with an unease which shifted from charming to irritable the longer he spoke with someone. He was eloquent, but remained quiet and anxious, hesitant - particularly towards women.

They boarded the train and Jim moved down the carriage to stand facing where Sarah sat, still unaware of her presence, until she caught his eye as the train approached Hammersmith. He looked towards her in a sudden double take, raising his eyebrows and lifting his nose to an angle like the first step of deciphering a punch line of a joke that needs too much work. It seemed an odd gesture, even to him.

Sarah watched him look out the window to the blurred platform as the train slowed down. He reached a hand into his pocket and pulled out a pen, which he studied and clicked on and off twice before returning it nervously to his pocket and stepping through the open, beeping doors. They walked separately to the office.

Peter's tube train shuddered from the west along the tracks towards Barons Court station. His best strategy was to start the week as if nothing had happened, arrive at the office early, and move beyond his outburst. That was the plan. He typed a Twitter status into his phone as he walked from the tube station to work, choosing his words with uncharacteristic caution to be deliberately mundane.

District Line borked. Read Metro all the way through. Spoiler alert: Sport.

He crossed Hammersmith Road and shook off the rain as he swiped his ID card through the turnstiles in the reception area of the NPL building. He was already fifteen minutes late, but he took the lift to the top floor to buy a coffee from the cafeteria and sat at a table while he checked his phone for emails before heading to his desk. He tapped his card on the reader of the door to the Editorial department, entering with what he hoped would be taken as a burst, making strides towards the newsdesk.

"OK people, what have we got?" he said as he approached, taking off his jacket. He placed it over the back of his chair.

Jim glanced over the top of his screen. He knew not to answer because it was a running joke which no longer required either a laugh or acknowledgement.

What they had was news stories off the wires. The bulletins came in through one cable and were published through another. Peter didn't make the decision about which reports were written by the journalists in the field and he didn't need to bark orders like a consulting physician in a cliché-ridden medical drama, but he thought it was funny when he did, partly because it made such little difference.

It would have been more fitting to ask "Is there anything we don't have?" because if fresh stories were being filed and weren't subsequently published then there *would* be cause for barking, aimed at the IT Department who would fix the newswire, unclogging the blockage which prevented the flow of news coverage to NPL's audience.

In the rare event of nothing being filed about an event, Peter would call his former colleagues at the newswire bureaux and ask if they were planning on covering the story.

Occasionally Peter would contact a reporter about a lead he had heard about on Twitter, Facebook or unofficial sources, and sometimes talk to his old bosses. "We're getting reports of a tree falling in a forest," he would say. "Do you have any audio?"

Peter would inform the bureau staff that his professional life was fine and that his career was going well, that online was where the excitement was, at the sharp end of an ever-accelerating news cycle - but he knew it didn't have the romance of his days as a correspondent.

His stint as an agency hack lasted just short of two years before he made the jump in 1996 to become an online editor. At times he regretted the move, having never felt the shallow glory of seeing his by-line next to an exotic foreign location. "Peter Beckenham, Cartegena." "Our man in Tallinn." "Dateline: Pretoria."

That was the romantic ideal, for him at least, in the eighteen months he spent with Reuters as an agency news correspondent before he moved to NPL. But his beat had been covering European political stories from Brussels, and it was as much as a twenty-three year old cub reporter could have hoped for. He once joined a press trip to St. Petersburg as part of an EU delegation, but that was as far as he was ever flung.

In some ways he was grateful for it. He didn't enjoy being in the spotlight as much as he liked being thought of as the person in it. At the age of thirty on a wet morning in Hammersmith, he wondered if a continued fourteen years in the field would have earned him postings in locations more exotic than Belgium, which in his mind was anywhere.

Jim was eight years younger than Peter, but that difference meant he had a purely new media background, joining NPL straight out of university in 1999. Words like "engagement" and "uniques" to describe editorial strategy and audience size were as natural to him as "print run" and "edition" were to newspaper journalists.

What have we got?

Peter knew how ridiculous it sounded but it raised a smirk out of some of the team and that was validation enough. What he meant was "*What are the real journalists saying and how quickly can we tell everyone else?*"

He was the editor of the country's biggest online news service, with web traffic exceeding the circulation of the paper editions of the New York Times, Daily Telegraph and Le Monde combined. In reality, neither question made much difference to the team responsible for producing NPL News.

Peter had been at the frontier of online news since the days of the web's pioneers. He had helped redefine reporting in the early days of the internet. The world of journalism had changed, and to some extent it was his fault. It no longer mattered who was earliest with the story, what counted most was where people read it first. The "first draft of history" was disposable because the second draft was only ninety seconds behind it, and it contained video.

Peter didn't see it as his place to make sense of the world - he would leave that to the newspapers. His team's role was to tell people what had happened while trying to make an honest living from the suffering of others.

This was something that he lost no sleep over, because he knew that without suffering he would be out of a job. There weren't enough celebrity weddings to provide his team of six journalists with enough material to run a news service.

Suffering, as he saw it, was a part of life. He understood this, and it was as much an element of human nature as the curiosity that makes people want to read about who has suffered and what caused it.

To Peter, pretending people didn't suffer was like imagining that a game of football would never end. He knew it would, and when the final whistle blew there would be a score and people would want to know the result.

He made sure people understood this when they took the job. When he interviewed Jim for the Deputy Editor role, Peter said: "Imagine a ferry sinks. Normally they float, but sometimes nature wins. When it does there are consequences and we tell people."

"I totally agree. We're providing a service," Jim said. He was specific about the *we're*, which he had said to evoke a solidarity with a team he hadn't joined yet. He knew that Peter would pick up on the creative visualisation, but he didn't expect to be challenged so quickly when Peter made his next point.

"Drug dealers also provide a service."

"Yes," said Jim smiling nervously, unsure where the conversation was headed. "Yes. I suppose they do."

"Drug dealers provide a harmful product."

"Absolutely," said Jim. "I agree."

Peter leaned forward and took a breath to think about how he was going to word what he had said a dozen times before. "A news report about suffering is not harmful," he said. "It may even prevent future disasters. Security may be improved, defences ramped up, aid flown in, pre-emptive measures taken."

Peter believed he was able to do his job because of the existence of suffering, but he was convinced he didn't cause any of it. "Whether we do our jobs or not, bad things will happen," he said. "We make a living *because* of bad things. A chef doesn't cause hunger and worry about making a living from it. We are journalists."

"The audience shouldn't feel guilty either," said Jim.

Peter liked him. "When can you start?"

The door to the Editorial department beeped and Karl walked into the large room, stopping to discuss sales figures at the commercially-focused channels that flanked his office. As Editorial Director, he ensured they brought in the money, which helped the loss-making, large audience sections like News survive. The Music channel took a share of the digital sales, Lifestyle had fashion advertising and shopping partners, Travel took a commission from bookings, but News had general advertising placements aimed at a broad, transient audience of no fixed demographic.

News was an expensive operation with unsociable staff hours and high fees for the newswire copy which fed it. Travel could hire more staff and double the amount of money they were making, whereas News could never be a success on the same commercial terms - a point Peter made regularly in many of the meetings he had with Karl.

In those exchanges, Karl would start off looking concerned and ask what Peter's team goals were and how he thought he could earn NPL more money. Peter would reply by asking if the sales team were placing enough ads on the News pages. "News is a tricky area," Karl would say. "You can't sponsor a plane crash."

"I could double the numbers in showbiz news if I dumbed it down a few notches," would be Peter's reply, knowing that went against the grain of NPL's highbrow target audience and the conversation would be brought to a close.

At the far end of the department, Karl laughed at something the Shopping Editor said and started walking again, past his office and down towards News.

"Peter, a word please?"

Peter stood up. "Any word in particular?" he said. He forced a smile.

"Actually two."

But he couldn't hold it.

The pair walked to Karl's office together. Peter took this as a bad sign. That and his boss's silence. If Karl had wanted to have a casual chat, Peter knew his boss would have walked over to News until he was close enough to call out to him and then head back to his office, expecting to be followed. Bad news was always preceded by Karl's physical proximity, to ease the discomfort of what he was reluctant to say next.

Peter closed the sliding door behind them and they sat down in the meeting area in front of Karl's desk. Peter waited for his boss to speak first.

Karl leaned forward until his elbows rested on the table and turned his palms up in an imploring manner before speaking.

"You know the social networking policies here, don't you?"

"Karl, man, look. I'm really - I can..."

Karl dropped his shoulders and sighed. He braced himself against the pity he felt for Peter's apology. Karl had considered leaving the company three weeks after his promotion because he couldn't balance out his professionalism with managing his former colleagues and, in this case, a friend. He also knew Peter was trying to push his buttons by calling him "man".

"This is going to go to HR, Peter. It has to. Too many people have seen it and things have to be done by the book. You've painted yourself into a corner, and you know what that makes?"

"Footprints?"

"Footprints, exactly. And you've got painty feet, Peter. Not me, not anyone else."

Peter thought about this for a second.

"This isn't advice - it's action, Peter, and there's going to be action taken. I'm telling you this before we go and see HR who said my next conversation with you should be with them present."

"Right." He hated Karl for a second and it flared within him briefly. Peter looked across the desk at the pictures of Karl's family and he understood that his boss had to do this.

Karl's tone softened. "Not *motherfucker*, Peter," he pleaded.

"I know," Peter said, shaking his head in disbelief at himself.

Karl wanted to ask for an explanation but he waited for Peter to talk.

"I was trying to be funny," he said, raising his voice at the end to imply the consequence.

Karl sighed through his nose. "You know how careful we had to be with the BNP thing," he said.

Peter had chosen to include the racist organisation in a list of political parties in a poll for the 2005 General Election. Word of its inclusion reached various white power forums, and supporters of the British National Party organised a campaign to vote in NPL's survey in large numbers, skewing the results to make it look like the BNP would receive twenty five per cent of the national vote. It didn't play out well with the audience or in the boardroom.

Karl looked at him sympathetically.

"So what's going to happen?" Peter asked.

"It's not good. Half the office follows you on Twitter."

"I deleted the update," said Peter.

"A lot of people saw it. And even if just one of your followers had - we're a media company. We work with the Government on internet security and child safety. We have partnerships with the BBC. The Daily Mail follows you."

"We're worried about the *Mail*?" said Peter. "They're bigger arseholes than me."

"People read the Daily Mail."

"What if my account had been hacked?"

"And the hacker stayed quiet for the rest of the weekend, and then tweeted about the District Line being stuffed? On your route, and from your phone?"

Peter knew that if Karl had been looking at his Twitter updates from that morning, it would have been because someone had told him to before the meeting. He figured that would make this, in HR terms, "the conversation", the purpose of which would allow Karl to go back to the Managing Director and say that he had "spoken with Peter who had admitted his wrongdoing and…"

Because there was always an *and*. Managers loved adding them to action points and filling them with constructive information and proactive measures their bosses hadn't asked for -

"I was seeing if anyone had searched for the language which was broadcast by the BBC," said Peter. "I'm sorry."

The "and" would be "and Peter apologised", which Karl hoped would be enough for everyone to move on.

Peter looked out the window for inspiration before turning back to Karl. "I'll apologise to anyone who needs to hear it."

"You can't apologise to the BBC."

"I picked out two words and instead of hitting Search, I clicked Send. I realised my mistake straight away," said Peter.

"So did seventeen thousand other people."

Peter was both surprised and flattered that Karl knew how many followers he had. Peter didn't point out how few followers would have actually seen the update. It wouldn't have helped him, because in the world of corporate media, policy was policy.

Peter was News Editor for the UK division of NPL, a bleached, white-bread internet service provider, with family values so strong that when the rival web service Valuenet launched, the board at the global headquarters in New York had told the PR team in London to register pornographic user names on the competitor's service in an attempt to demonstrate the immorality of an unmoderated internet.

NPL had even appointed a Head of Editorial Standards to make sure editors didn't publish pictures of people pointing guns straight at the camera, or images which showed people enjoying alcohol or two women kissing.

When Britney Spears kissed Madonna on stage at the MTV Awards, Peter was advised not to use the picture, despite the company having an active non-discrimination hiring policy and a Gay and Lesbian community channel. The problem with the picture, he was told, was that it portrayed lesbians in a physical act. Single sex relationships were fine, she explained, as long as they weren't depicted in a sexual context, and because Britney and Madonna weren't *actual* lesbians, the kiss was a display for the titillation of the audience. The Head of Editorial Standards told the News team "the publication of these images is an issue to which NPL will not be a party".

The edict was met by a long, disdainful silence, which Peter broke. "A lesbian party?"

That led to a verbal warning.

Karl was waiting for Peter to speak.

"So what happens now?" he asked.

He had visions of the long walk back to his desk, and the IT department suspending his network access, which would make it hard for him to pretend he was working until the office cleared for lunch when he could pack up and walk through the department in sight of the people eating at their desks. He imagined they would watch him walk past carrying his belongings in a box with a trophy sticking out over the cardboard. He wondered if he actually *had* a trophy, because in his imagination there was always a trophy.

"You don't see anyone from HR here, do you?" said Karl.

He thought he had a bottle opener somewhere. He wondered if he could fashion a makeshift plinth out of a hole-punch.

Karl raised inquisitive eyebrows and stuck his neck out in a small jut. It was almost Gallic. Peter wondered if he had picked it up from his wife, the sumptuous Anne-Sophie. She reminded Peter of Juliette Binoche and he wondered what she saw in Karl. He was a nice enough man, but at barely forty had a disproportionate amount of hair in his ears and tiny hands for a man who claimed to play the upright bass.

He had met her at several staff parties and loved how she said their last name, Howard. "Ow'ar-de." Like an arrow being shot through a pile of leaves.

"No," said Peter. "I don't."

"Then this is just an informal chat at this stage."

"OK."

"Right. And I'm sending you to Liverpool."

"Doesn't that require some kind of written warning?"

"I'd like you to go up with Jim tomorrow to meet The Echo for the local newspaper project. You can stay in the company apartment."

NPL had decided that internet news, which both covered and reached the whole world, should also be local. People would "engage", as Jim would say, with their regional coverage through their internet service provider, which would publish local updates from regional newspapers, council services and community forums which had less of an online presence than a national medium like NPL.

Peter didn't want to go, but he knew Karl would present this to HR as having relieved Peter temporarily of his duties, giving him a few days away while he thought about his mistake and perhaps considered his position and commitment to the company.

"You know there's a civil war starting in Cote d'Ivoire?" said Peter. "No one else is going to run it and we have a head start on the coverage. The artwork's all done and I have a contact ready for live audio."

"Peter, your tweet could have been very damaging to the company. You're an excellent journalist and I don't doubt your editorial judgement for a second, but I can't let any of my staff become a liability."

He stood up and moved towards the door. Peter followed.

"But I'll miss the war..." he pleaded in a comic whine. He looked around Karl's office for trophies.

"Well, maybe you'll start one in Liverpool."

5
Tuesday 29 June 2010
Euston Station, London

Jim was waiting at 8:15 as arranged, outside the Starbucks by Platform 12. Peter looked up from his BlackBerry as he moved through a wave of commuters and pointed his nose towards his colleague before returning to his messages while he walked.

Jim smiled and tried to wave with three fingers while holding up two cups of coffee. He extended a cup to his boss. "Morning," said Peter, taking the cup. "Thanks. Do we have a platform yet?"

"Five. Right this way."

Jim liked to help people. Peter thought that Jim needed to feel the appreciation that he was going out of his way for their convenience whether they needed it or not. It annoyed Peter, and he suspected that Jim, for all his niceties, put his position of helper before the comfort of others. Peter could have bought his own coffee, or he may not have wanted one, but he knew Jim would feel compelled to provide one anyway.

The problem was compounded by Peter's aversion to being provided for. He had been at boarding school from the age of ten, his father was in the oil business, his mother was a writer, and they both travelled too much with work to provide a stable home environment. His world of dorm rooms and canteens had nurtured him into a creature of self-reliance, although one with a need for attention due to emotional neglect. In a petri dish under the right conditions, it was a perfect environment for breeding a journalist.

Right this way, Peter thought, sneering. Fucking helpers. Always smiling over you. Always with the questions apart from the obvious one about asking if they can be your mother. Always wondering aloud about your needs.

Peter wasn't a morning person. He refused the offer of a newspaper twice on the way to the train.

NPL's Technical Development team was based in an office in the newly renovated Pier Head area of Liverpool. Alexis DeSousa was named Chief Technology Officer after founding the UK operation in 1995. He started in a rented office space in Bootle with the consent of the company's head office in New York. With six month's work and a plane ticket from Merseyside to Manhattan he had convinced the world's largest media company that he could give them the technical development, support and manpower it needed to become the biggest internet service provider in Europe.

Since those early days, the technology department moved into a modern office overlooking the river where it employed forty developers, not including two call centres in Warrington, and Alexis had bought himself a six bedroom house in Cheshire.

Peter had been to the Liverpool office a dozen times while overseeing the many News channel redesigns and he liked Alexis' entrepreneurial spirit almost as much as his Greek/Scouse accent. "Grouse", Peter called it, and he used the term affectionately, coming from the soft spot he had for the city where three of his four grandparents were born.

But Peter found the man's pride hard to bear. Alexis boasted about the gains of his hard work, and Peter couldn't resist cutting him down to size. On one visit he stood in Alexis's office and was made to take in the view over the Mersey in a scene played out for Peter's admiration.

"Just look at that," said Alexis. "This started out in a warehouse, and now look at this view. The history in that water..."

"You've come a long way, Alexis," said Peter, "but remember that's Wales on the other side."

Alexis turned from the dark river to look at him.

"Guess you can't have it all," said Peter. He tapped Alexis on the shoulder and walked to the kitchen.

The company kept a serviced, two-bedroom apartment by Lime Street train station for employees to use when they came up from London to work with the developers. It allowed directors over from the US to visit the Liverpool office without having to make it back to Hammersmith on the same day, or book into a hotel when they worked on week-long projects. Although they weren't visiting the riverside office on this trip, Peter and Jim were given the keys to the flat that wasn't being used.

Peter spent the train journey fending off Jim's proposals for tea and refusing offers of newspaper loans while he worked on the pitch to The Echo. The aim was to convince the publisher that an online newsdesk in London owned by a company based in New York was best placed to publish news for the biggest daily newspaper on Merseyside. The strategy made no sense to him, but he didn't lose any sleep over it after an Italian meal at a restaurant on the Albert Dock. He stopped off for a pint on the way

back to the apartment and Jim continued the taxi ride
back on his own.

6
Wednesday 30 June 2010
Liverpool

Peter woke from a deep sleep unsure of many things, including when he had last felt so rested and how Jim had bought the eggs he could smell frying.

He padded down the hallway and stepped into the shower. The tap shuddered as he turned it on and he eased the water to as hot as he could stand to loosen up the muscles tightened by an unfamiliar bed.

Peter dressed and went to the living area where Jim was making breakfast. He had already showered and was standing over a frying pan at the cooker, dressed in an ensemble of suit trousers, work shoes and a pyjama shirt.

"OK," said Jim, turning around, "so that was weird."

Toast popped up. There was a plastic supermarket bag on the kitchen table.

"Um," said Peter, pointing lazily at Jim, "Why the pyjama shirt?"

"I feel comfortable. I was up early," said Jim.

Peter looked at the bag. "But you've been out."

"I didn't go *out* in my pyjama shirt."

"No, of course not, that would have been stupid."

"Yes."

"But you went to the shops and changed back into it."

"Well, yes. It's comfortable, and I'm not going to fry eggs in my work shirt."

Peter pictured Jim bare-chested at the cooker and shuddered inside. He needed a coffee. "I guess not," he said. "What's weird?"

"What?"

"You said 'That was weird.'"

"Right." Jim's shirt was a flannel tartan in checked blues and greens, untucked over his pinstripe suit trousers. He slid an egg from the pan onto a piece of toast and held the plate as he spoke. "We turned the taps on at the same time."

"Oh."

"In different rooms. At exactly the same time."

"OK."

Jim put a plate on the table for Peter. "Oh no, you can't just brush this one off," he said. "That's an amazing coincidence."

"It's not an *amazing coincidence*. It's morning and we're on a schedule. We're both getting ready and that involves water consumption."

"Oh my god."

"What?" said Peter as he stepped towards the fridge.

"Right after it happened, I thought about telling you about it when you came in, and I imagined I did and that was your exact reply. Those exact same words. Holy Moses, Peter."

Peter closed the fridge and scanned the kitchen surfaces. "Are you finished now?" he said.

"OK, this is too weird." Jim put the plate on the table.

"Look. You would have assumed that would be my reaction, because I'm a confirmed sceptic and you're familiar with how I speak because we've been working together for eleven years, occasionally travelling together on business, and staying in shared accommodation."

"You're still doing it!"

Jim stared at him in shock as Peter opened the door of the fridge for a second time and spoke into it. "Where's the juice?"

His colleague's face turned white with eyes grotesquely large. He looked like a beflannelled squid.

"Peter. The juice is already on the table. It's like I knew you were going to say that."

"You need to calm down, OK?" Peter sat at the table in front of his egg on toast. "This is not a coincidence. It's early. It's been a long week. But turning the taps on at the same time is not a coincidence. We set our alarms last night, and when we woke up, one of us was going to have a shower and the other was going to make some coffee. That was always going to happen."

"Not like this, Peter. This is too perfect."

"No it's fucking not! What would have been weird is if either of us had neither showered nor boiled a kettle this morning, if you were sitting eating toast without a drink and if I had thought, 'You know what? I'm not going to wash before our meeting.'" He waved a laden fork at Jim. "*That* would have been weird." He took a mouthful.

"The water? Your reply? The *orange juice*? That's too much."

Peter shook his head and swallowed hard and quickly. "For fuck's sake, Jim." Jim remained standing, transfixed and indignant by the table. "I had a shower, I spoke, I wanted some juice. That's it. I think you need to calm down and put your shirt on."

"I'm just saying that you can't brush this off, like you're Mister blimming, I dunno, Mister Brightstuff or something."

"What does that even *mean*?"

"Well, you're," said Jim with an uncomfortable shrug, "you can be a little, you know..." he continued, raising his eyebrows, " - and I'm not the *only* one." He looked at Peter sympathetically, and, satisfied that he had made his point, returned to his bedroom.

Peter thought the meeting at The Echo that afternoon had gone well, mostly because no one pointed out the obvious flaws in the proposal, including having one technical support team working across two different editorial systems, production staff with no regional knowledge of the North West, advertisers who weren't interested in national exposure outside of their own market and the uncertainty of the size or interest of the expat audience - but it was polite and civil and Peter was glad to be out of the Hammersmith office.

After a quick sandwich they walked to Lime Street station and boarded the early evening train back to London.

Jim sat next to Peter and looked at him staring out the window as the train pulled out.

"Liverpool," said Jim.

Peter sighed. It was more out of resignation that Jim was going to make a point he didn't need to, but Jim had taken it as wistful which matched the mood of what he was about to say. Peter knew he would have said it anyway, but Jim appreciated the encouragement.

"Land of your fathers," he said.

"Land of *my* fathers," Peter corrected him.

"That's what I said. It is the land of your fathers, isn't it?"

"It is, but the expression is 'land of my fathers'."

"But isn't *your* family from Liverpool?"

"You see," Peter put his cup of tea down on the table, "no one says that. No one would say 'land of your fathers'."

"It is, though."

"I know it is, Jim. But no one does that. It's like you're providing a narrative for my emotions. It's just odd. It's like offering someone chewing gum on the tube."

"That was a nice gesture." Jim performed random acts of kindness which were more random than kind. Londoners were especially wary.

"It's just... it's odd."

"I don't see why."

Jim looked at the fingerprint smears on the window.

"This is your second time in Liverpool in as many months," said Peter.

Jim took a sip of tea.

"A nice cup of tea..." said Peter,

Jim nodded and opened the newspaper.

"Catching up on the day's news..." said Peter,"...to get the full account of the current events..."

Jim looked up. "Sorry," he said, "do you want to read it?"

"No!" said Peter. "Isn't that annoying?".

"Isn't what annoying?"

"Me! Just then! Giving a running commentary of how you're feeling and what you're doing."

"I didn't notice."

"How can you not notice?"

"I just didn't."

Peter shook his head in despair and watched the countryside roll by as the train carried them south.

Jim looked at the sticker on the window. It had a pair of headphones and a mobile phone crossed out.

"Quiet carriage," said Jim.

7
Thursday 1 July 2010
Hammersmith

The rain floated down, soft in the air, dampening Peter's suit jacket as he walked. It moved towards him in a thick mist and he thought he would have stayed drier if he stood still, which seemed a better option than meeting Karl and Human Resources for a meeting about his Twitter update later that morning.

Jim was already at his desk when Peter walked in. Jim watched him take off his jacket and put it on the back of his chair, adjusting the empty shoulders in measured, almost theatrical movements.

"Bet you saw that coming," said Peter.

"What?" said Jim.

"My desk, my chair? Oooh." He made hocus pocus hands.

Jim looked back at his screen and clicked something.

"Coffee?" Peter said.

Jim kept his eyes on the screen and nodded to the far end of the room. "In the kitchen."

"I mean do you want one?"

Jim looked up. "No thank you," he said emphatically.

He clicked again before returning his eyes to his screen.

In the kitchen, Peter pushed the coffee button and wondered whether to switch the lead story, a dull but worthy political survey, for the earthquake or something light but popular. A 7.5 was big, but Heather Mills was back in the headlines and she always did the numbers.

Earlier that week the Creative Director, an overdressed man called Jonathan Cahill who looked like an underfed Elvis Costello, had set page view targets for all the channels at NPL, and the News figures could be achieved with an accompanying drop in editorial standards.

The Learning channel would never meet its revised objectives, but as Peter might have put it, all News had to do was throw another couple of David Beckhams on the fire.

Learning was run by Sarah Copland, one of several US imports at the company who had worked in the New York office before being offered a job in London. She sat two desk rows beyond News, in front of a small meeting area at the far end of the Editorial department. She knew little about current affairs beyond her own views, which always extended across the room when a big story hit.

On the crest of breaking events, she tended to wander into the middle of the hub of the six desks that formed the News channel to talk to Peter and discuss his opinions on the latest story.

"Who could *do* that? Their poor mother." She sounded old fashioned sometimes, especially for an American and she had a Maryland accent that Peter could distinguish from New York or Philadelphia. She seasoned her sepia phrases with words like "hark" and "mightn't", to which her looks added a charm.

Peter was drawn to accents. He loved to place a lilt or turn of phrase and pick people up on them. Those too obscure or subtle for most English ears gave him more delight when he correctly guessed where the speaker called home. Montreal, Pennsylvania, West Berkshire.

He liked words, too, and enjoyed using the right ones when others struggled. "*Defiled*, you mean?" he would say when it was the exact terminology the person had been looking for.

He sometimes employed the *wrong* word when he had the satisfaction of knowing he was wrong. When a colleague brought him a cup of coffee he could announce its arrival as "awesome" and take a moment of private amusement in knowing there was nothing awesome about it.

Sarah's vocabulary suited her eyes, with Photoshopped whites around a lively hazel set in a look of tender sympathy. Light brown hair hung straight almost to her shoulders with a fringe that always looked like she was growing it out.

She was average height and curvy to the extent that she wanted to be slimmer but no one who didn't know her Body Mass Index would have assumed she was carrying the weight. Peter thought her figure gave her an appeal which was cute yet sensual, with a graceful, mature control.

Beneath her sober nature ran a dry sense of humour and she enjoyed Peter's cutting jibes about her interrupting the journalists when a story broke.

She once said about striking tube drivers: "They are so overpaid. I should do that."

Peter replied, "Or your *own* job?" - to which he thought she had taken offence, although he noticed the odds didn't lengthen on their seemingly coincidental trips to the kitchen for coffee.

Peter poured himself a cup while she stood next to him with an empty mug.

"So how was Liverpool?" she asked.

Peter hadn't mentioned that he would be away, and he guessed she had asked after him while he was gone.

She didn't wait for an answer. "Lunch later if you fancy it?"

And she said "fancy it". There was a charm to the way her accent wrapped around English phrases. Peter wondered where this might lead him.

He threw a spoon in the sink and was friendly when he said, "No thanks, I'll get something here."

"You're terrible to Jim," she said with a note of concern that he thought might be flirtatious.

"He's all right," he said. "You think so?"

There was a lingering as she leaned across to the kettle, like her feet were rooted to the floor as she reached to push the button for a drink, and she was standing closer to him than to her cup. Peter wondered if it was a choice she wanted him to notice she had made.

He observed the subtle angle she held, made more noticeable by the vertical drop in her loose shirt, punctuated by hints of an intimate geography, which unfurled his imagination.

"Jim's a good person. You should be nicer to him."

Peter felt a twinge of guilt on two fronts. "He's such an easy hit. He makes himself a target."

"No one does that. No one *asks* to be picked on." Sarah's voice dropped and hastened as she urged a nod behind him.

Peter said loudly, "And he's right behind me, isn't he?"

Sarah looked into her cup to hide her embarrassment.

Jim took it as a joke and didn't assume he had been the topic of the conversation, because it was something Peter would do often.

Peter caught Sarah's eye, turned to Jim and said, "I might grab lunch later in the cafeteria. Want to come along?"

"I might do," said Jim, "I made a cheese sandwich at home but I left it in my fridge."

Peter made a poor attempt to stifle a snort and looked at Sarah with a mocking nonchalance.

Jim saw her give Peter an admonishing smile. Indignant, Jim shot them both an accusing look and said, "Oh, like you've never forgotten cheese."

Peter looked into the middle distance with a sense of accomplishment. He walked slowly towards his desk alone. "...like you've never forgotten cheese...," he said to himself.

Sarah's voice lilted behind him: "Hey Jim. How are you?"

Peter led with the earthquake, and put Heather Mills second, followed by the previous night's football. At eleven o'clock Karl called Peter into his office. Sally Van Der Kamp from Human Resources sat at the table at the front of the room, behind her printed notes. There were bullet points on the sheets, but Peter didn't allow his gaze to rest long enough to read the details. He and Karl took their places at the round table, each at an equal distance like card players. Sally said good morning, softened in a Dutch American brogue.

"So you understand the purpose of this meeting is to discuss your communication on the evening of the twenty fifth of June regarding a message you sent out on the social networking site Twitter."

"A 'tweet'," thought Peter. He was baffled at how NPL's Personnel department knew less about the internet than the Facilities team, despite being in charge of screening applications for every new hire in Editorial.

"I do," he said.

"In that communication you said 'BBC motherfuckers' which you're aware is a breach of the company's standards of behaviour and also its social networking policy."

Peter cringed inwardly at the sound of the word.

"Yes I did - I am. I was shocked that the BBC had broadcast the words and I looked for the term on Twitter and accidentally typed it into the Update field instead of the Search box, publishing a status that should have been a search query. I have discussed this with Karl."

Karl nodded to Sally. Peter thought Sally was attractive; a symphony in Boden clothing and dental veneers, country farmhouse meets urban chic. He looked at the skin of her shoulder under her crocheted top. For him it stirred a heady cocktail of contradictions - a sensual sensitivity, upmarket yet downtown and tantalising, dowdy but rowdy.

The choice of fabric, he thought, said a lot about a woman's sexuality, and with crochet it could go either way, but on the right body it was defiant and bold. To him it was the tweed of the late noughties. He thought about the phrase *late noughties*.

Karl looked away from Sally and turned towards Peter, deep in thought with his attention held by the finger-sized holes in the black wool hovering above her left clavicle. He wasn't aware even that he was breathing until he heard Karl's voice which caused him to take in air with a serious sniff to punctuate his alertness.

"I spoke to Peter the next morning," said Karl, "and due to the nature of his comments and his sizeable following on the network, I advised Jonathan that we call this meeting and have a formal discussion."

Peter didn't want to deny Karl the privilege of the duty of management in name checking the boss. He knew Karl was simply doing his job when he brought the matter to the Creative Director's attention.

Sally looked at Peter. "Is there anything you would like to add?"

"No, I think that covers it. I was stupid. *It* was stupid. And I shouldn't have written what I did."

"Great," said Karl. Peter could tell he was trying to wrap up the meeting.

Sally looked at Karl, who made it clear he wasn't going to say any more by turning away from Peter and raising his eyebrows at her.

"Karl and I will discuss further and inform you of the outcome," she said. "You are free to go."

Peter stood up. "Thanks," he said. He shut the door behind him and walked to the kitchen area.

Sarah was making herself a cup of soup.

"Just boiled?" he said.

She winced. "There's only enough for one."

"Fine," he said, exasperated, "*go on* then. Have it *all*."

She looked hurt.

"I'm joking," he said.

She relaxed. "So have you had the meeting?"

With comedic study, he watched her pour all the boiling water into her mug.

"The meeting," she pressed. "I saw Sally from HR down here earlier."

She stirred her soup and he looked on disapprovingly. He shook his head at the mug in disbelief as she put the empty kettle back on its stand. She smiled at him as he continued the bit, which he broke to smile back.

He gave her a quizzical look. "What's the deal with crochet?" he said.

"Crochet?"

"Yeah. 'I wrapped up but I don't want to be warm.' They're string vests for the middle classes. It's fishnet knitwear."

"Not all crochet is revealing, Peter."

"The good stuff is. Why go for wool at all? Why not go for a tighter weave? Or a chunky knit? What's your soup?"

"Cream of mushroom," she said.

"That's a good soup. And yes I did."

"You creamed a mushroom?"

"No, I had the meeting."

"Oh right," said Sarah with soft, sunken, northeastern seaboard vowels, "with Sally?"

"Sally in the crochet, and Karl."

"You don't begrudge him, do you?"

"Karl? Not a bit. The thought of him in crochet..." He made a face of mild revulsion.

"It's a defence mechanism, isn't it?"

"...And yet it's alluring and keeps you *warm*."

"Your humour, I mean. This means you're in trouble."

"The jury's out."

He reached for the kettle as Karl walked into the kitchen behind him. Sarah looked at Peter and nodded towards their boss.

"And he's standing right behind me, isn't he?"

Sarah smiled at Karl.

Peter turned towards his boss as he took a mug from the shelf. "All rise," said Peter.

"OK there?" said Karl.

"Yeah," said Peter.

"Good."

"I was, er, about to fill the kettle," said Peter, clearly, for Sarah to hear. "I wondered if you were also going to make a hot drink and whether I needed to put more water in." He looked at Sarah. She smiled as she blew across the top of her mug with the spoon still in it. It was mid-summer though rainy, but she held the mug with both hands. *Cupping*, Peter thought.

"No, thank you," said Karl, "I was just checking in."

"Thanks," said Peter. "I'm fine." He wanted Karl to be reassured.

"OK," said Karl. He tapped his pockets and returned to his office.

"See?" Peter said to her, "One big happy family."

"Really?"

"Compared to mine, yeah."

He filled the kettle and flicked the switch.

"How are things with Jim?" she said.

Jim would often say things that left people perplexed. He was odd in a nice way, but just too far past normal to be endearing, and sometimes as charmless as a hotel room carpet.

No one thing he did was particularly strange in itself, but put together they seemed off-key. He would shave in the office, but only occasionally, perhaps one day every three weeks, in the middle of the afternoon, when he had no plans for the evening, which was most evenings.

He would offer food to colleagues - something that seemed normal when you told someone and odd when you explained it. Anyone who went home and said to his or her partner: "Jim offered me food today" would hear the reply: "That's nice". Then they would explain that Jim offered them a peanut by saying: "Would you care for a peanut?"

Usually, in delivery of the offer, Jim would act as if he had suddenly caught himself being rude by eating and not being gracious first, so he prefaced his generosity by pulling himself up on his lack of manners, so the offer of a peanut, *a* peanut, would be made with a full mouth and begin with a startled: "Mhmm. Sorry, I'm sorry..." The offer would come while the person was talking to someone to whom the offer would rarely extend.

Peter took a mug from the shelf, spooned in a measure of coffee and filled his cup. "Same as ever. Things with Jim are: ...Jim-my. They are Jimsical. Jimbiotic."

"He looks up to you, you know," said Sarah.

Peter looked over to Jim's desk and back to Sarah.

He interrupted his first sip. "We're in our thirties," he said, "our heroes should all be dead. And if they're not, they aren't talking about being heroes in Hammersmith office kitchens."

"I didn't say you were his hero."

"But he looks up to me, right?" said Peter hopefully.

She smiled and finished stirring her soup and tapped the rim of her mug twice with the spoon before putting it down by the sink. "You need to be careful with him."

Peter picked up the spoon, hit his mug twice, put it down emphatically by the sink and said: "*You* need to be careful with him."

Her smile grew while she shook her head in mock despair. They left the kitchen together.

"I'm still *your* hero, though, right?"

"I don't know," she said, "are you dead?"

"Only on the inside."

"You're funny."

"...Where I'm also crying." He made a sad face.

"Very good."

As they approached News, Peter said, "I might take you up on that lunch."

"Um, OK," said Sarah, wondering if his suggestion had been influenced by the intimacy or comfortable warmth of their conversation.

"Great," said Peter. He stopped walking and pointed to his desk and shrugged. "Well, this is my stop. I guess I'll see you later."

Sarah nodded and was about to walk on when Peter turned to Jim.

"Jim, are you heading out at lunch at all today?"

Jim looked up and smiled at Sarah before answering. "I'm not sure I am. I'm busy for a while. I might go for a late one though, yes."

"Great, mind if I borrow your raincoat?"

"My raincoat?"

"It's raining six kinds of bastards out there and I've just got this." He looked down at his suit jacket.

"Sarah and I are going out early and since you're hanging around I was wondering…"

"…Sure." Jim, perplexed and forsaken, took the jacket off the back of his chair and handed it to Peter.

"Thanks." He put it on and looked at Sarah. "Ready?"

"Now?" she said. "Me?"

"Well Jim's not coming."

"You have my coat," said Jim.

"Yeah thanks a lot," said Peter. He turned back to Sarah. "At your leisure."

Jim would later write about the exchange in his blog. In his version, he would be the perplexed observer of an office character called "Thoughtless Colleague" who featured in a number of posts about corporate life.

Jim portrayed himself on the website, which he called The Penultimate Bastion, as someone who had more patience and strength of character than Peter gave him credit for.

Peter was a regular reader, and, under a pseudonym, an occasional commenter on The Bastion. He didn't know if Jim was aware that Peter visited it, and neither of them ever mentioned the website.

Peter was amused that Thoughtless Colleague was widely resented by Jim's hundred or so readers. He would himself sometimes give Jim advice on how to deal with him, but Jim never acted on it.

Jim also wrote about human rights issues, a cause for which he saw himself as a whistle blower, and his campaigns occasionally gained support on Facebook.

He would also write about an American teacher who worked at a newspaper, a national daily undisclosed because he said he also worked there. It was a good cover up because if the site were to attract unwelcome interest, people would assume the author was an anonymous print journalist, "inkies" to his online colleagues, and not someone who worked in digital media.

Jim didn't hide his feelings for his colleague de plume, whom he called Cindy. Peter guessed he chose the name because it sounded American, and he liked the sound of her. He knew Jim was attracted to Sarah, but it never came across in real life.

He thought Jim was a good writer, and his descriptions of her made her sound less refined, but his muse's grace and intelligence shone through in her playful eloquence. Jim's conversations with her were kept to short exchanges of pleasantries and conversations confined to subjects of office life including re-organisations, furnishings, the cold that was going around, strip lighting and outbreaks of pregnancy among colleagues.

This came up when the three of them were in the lift one morning on the way up to Editorial on the sixth floor.

"There must be something in the water," Jim said to Sarah.

"Jizz," said Peter, standing behind them. "I couldn't help but eavesdrop."

Jim turned around.

"Don't look at *me*," said Peter.

The doors opened and Sarah walked out. Jim looked disapprovingly at Sarah, who was stifling a smile.

8
Friday 2 July 2010
Hammersmith

One of the privileges of working on the newsdesk for Peter was that the television was always on. Breaking news would wash over his colleagues in a tide of events as they unfolded. Sport was shown when an event was newsworthy, and group stages of the World Cup in South Africa at the end of the week had his non-News colleagues craning their necks towards the action as they walked past. England had been dumped out of the tournament by Germany, giving everyone the chance to watch subsequent world-class football instead, and that afternoon Holland was playing Brazil.

Karl walked over to News and stood in front of the television next to Peter and Jim. "What's the score?" he asked Jim.

"Two one" said Peter, raising his mug to his lips without taking his eyes from the match.

"Ah," said Karl.

Peter flinched at a hard tackle.

Karl took a short breath and asked, "Who's playing?"

Peter looked at him.

"Brazil and the Netherlands," said Jim.

Karl nodded. "Peter. Can I have a word?"

Peter narrowed his eyes at Karl. "One or two?"

Karl smiled and walked back to his office.

Peter glanced at Jim's trousers. "Hmm. Chinos."

"Chinos. What?"

"Just it's a bit late for chinos."

"What do you mean late? It's the middle of summer."

"Yes, but not summer *1997*."

Jim looked at his choice of trousers as Peter walked past him to Karl's office.

He closed the door behind him. "What's up?"

"Good, look - we're having a rejig."

"Again? Last one was eighteen months ago."

Staff restructures happened at least every two years. Peter had reported in to seven different bosses in the fourteen years he had worked there. Each time a new manager came in he had to justify his own importance, followed by that of his team, and although there had been a couple of casualties in the Editorial department, News was left largely alone. Despite low revenues compared to the high audience figures, Peter ran a channel the company considered worth funding, particularly when page views numbered ten million a day.

"The US has handed down some targets and we need to cut our costs. I think it's the right thing to do."

Peter knew Karl didn't think it was the right thing to do. If he did he would have explained the bigger picture to show his support. Peter didn't really care, after having already survived multiple reshuffles of varying magnitudes as well as their aftershocks.

Peter thought that if Karl were to make him redundant, his length of service would net him enough money to fund a year off at least. And if NPL wanted him to stay, he was confident he would deliver the page views, whichever strategic direction they pointed him in.

"You've been here for how long now?" asked Karl.

"Fourteen years."

"How are you finding it?"

"Google Maps." He couldn't help himself. "It's OK. I love News and I like the people I work with - and for. I come to work every day, and it's OK."

Peter wasn't going to put a varnish on his attitude, or amplify his responsibility for an eighth reorganisation. He chuckled to himself. "Morgan Freeman," he said.

"What is?"

He shut his eyes tight, and then opened them. If thoughts were literally trains, Peter had a habit of starting them in the middle carriages, and out loud. He would assume the listener knew what he had been imagining. He also blinked hard when he pulled himself up on this quirk.

"Morgan Freeman. Shawshank Redemption?" said Peter. "When Red is in what turns out to be his last parole hearing, he's tired and he thinks whatever's going to happen will happen anyway, so after previous hearings in front of a variety of panels over the years, all of them resulting in failed appeals, he's resigned to his fate and he says to the chairman: 'So you go on and stamp your form, sonny, and stop wasting my time.'"

Karl smiled, and hesitated. "What if you could influence the outcome?"

"To be honest, I don't particularly know if I would want to stay."

"That's not what I meant," said Karl.

Peter checked the closed door behind him. "Oh," he said, suddenly interested, "if I chose to leave, you mean?"

"Fourteen years is a long time."

"It's a stretch."

Peter knew selective redundancies in the past had been agreed before the staff consultation processes had begun, and he didn't think the company would try to keep any senior manager or editor who didn't want to stay.

"Have a think about what you want to do," said Karl.

He didn't know what he wanted to do. As much as he enjoyed his work, he loved being a journalist and working in digital news. NPL, like hundreds of other news services on the web, put the emphasis on speed above context, and information over knowledge. He had stressed to his team the need to get a story up early and expand upon it later. Publish first, and publish often.

Unlike newspapers, the internet had no deadline because it was always the deadline. There was the post-publish intention to develop a story with picture galleries, write a background piece and pick up the phone for a pop-out quote, but usually once a story was published another event would break, one which also needed to go live as soon as possible, and news would flow relentlessly.

It was journalism without analysis and they were a production unit. There was no shame in that for Peter. He was happy being a curator - a producer instead of a creator. He thought of all the great producers like George Martin, Quincy Jones and Brian Eno. They made a valid contribution to the art form without writing the songs. He was certain the soundscape of people's lives would be different without them, but he wondered if Phil Spector had ever wanted to pick up a horn once or twice and write something.

Peter went back to his desk and considered how to shape his chance into a something that might resemble a destiny.

That afternoon his phone rang.

"Peter. Jean Claude."

Jean Claude Charbonneau had been Peter's second boss at NPL, Head of Editorial from 1998 to mid-2000, until he took redundancy and moved to Bahrain to edit Gulf Daily News, the country's biggest English language paper. The large tax-free salary was well deserved for a man whose eye for a story was unmatched.

He relaunched the Gulf Daily website a year later and always seemed too big for the role until he met his calling as Editor of Al Jazeera's English service in Dubai.

He was a tall man in his early forties, thick hair and a serious expression at odds with his relaxed nature. He was quick to smile and had an upmarket, classic sense of dress that bordered on dapper.

"JC, how the deuce. Are you in town?"

"I am. I'm visiting the children next week. They break up for summer on Wednesday so I thought I would come to England first."

Jean Claude's family lived in Paris where his wife Celine wanted the children to go to school. She lived with them in the 16th Arrondissement where she returned to teaching while he worked in the Middle East. "I live tax-free, we have paid off the mortgage and she hates me anyway, so it's good, no?" he said.

No, or at least, *not completely*, thought Peter, who had only heard one side of the story. He wasn't sure if the relationship broke up before or after Jean Claude had the affair, but the marriage was nearing an end. Work endured, so did parenthood, and as far as Peter could tell Jean Claude was enjoying a second freedom.

"I have plans at the weekend in Brighton," said Jean Claude, "but I was wondering if you wanted to come to Denmark Street with me and look at guitars."

"It's three o'clock on a Friday. I'd love to, but I'm at work."

Both Peter and Jean Claude were guitarists of an ability that could most kindly be called enthusiastic. The thought of running expensive Stratocasters through thick Marshall tube amplifiers tempted Peter but he was needed in the office.

"Ah, too bad," said Jean Claude. "I was hoping we could to stick it to the man."

"Jean Claude, you run Al Jazeera English, the most influential broadcaster in the Middle East. Your wife teaches economics at a private school and I'm in charge of the UK's biggest online channel for the world's largest media company. I'm pretty fucking sure we *are* the man."

Jean Claude laughed. "OK, OK, well, maybe yes. Are you free this evening?"

"Absolutely."

Peter took the train into town after work, intending to ask Jean Claude's advice about him weathering another reshuffle or leaving the company. Either way, Peter knew he wanted to remain a journalist and he was grateful that he didn't have a marriage to risk in its pursuit.

They met at a pub off Great Portland Street, away from the shoppers and the crowds of the West End bars. It hosted an after work crowd, a few locals and some casual evening diners. Jean Claude and Peter valued bars by their clientele and they found a table where they could sit and talk quietly.

After checking his phone messages, Jean Claude started talking to a woman at the table next to him while Peter went to order the drinks. From the bar, Peter heard Jean Claude say the words "Dubai" followed by his own name. Jean Claude's voice trailed off and the woman laughed.

Peter returned to the table where Jean Claude was holding court using nothing more than a grin. "This is him," he said, "this is Peter Beckenham."

Peter said hello to the woman and looked at her half empty drink as he put two pints of beer down on the table. He didn't need a wing man - or want one.

"Peter, Julie. Julie, Peter. I will return in two minutes."

Jean Claude stood up and scanned the room. He pointed with his thumb at the new drink and said thank you to Peter.

"Thank *you*," said Peter with a sarcasm he hoped only his friend would detect.

Jean Claude walked off intently and Peter sat down at his table.

"So you're a journalist," she said.

"Someone has to be."

She was young, in her early twenties, with jet-black wavy hair brushing the top of her vintage summer dress. She was voluptuous. Peter thought if she were stretching she wouldn't have looked out of place on the nose of a WWII bomber.

"What do *you* do?" he asked

"I'm in design."

To those in the media, this was a broad term, ranging from picture desk to page layout or digital product delivery.

"Right. What - graphics? Fashion? Production?"

It sounded rude to him as soon as he said it. Sometimes when Peter talked to people, he would watch their expressions change after he spoke. Their reaction was a sign that his delivery was disjointed from his thoughts or intentions. He knew they were right, and it happened so often that he spent a lot of time explaining what he meant or apologising. This time he spotted it, but the questions had already been delivered with scattergun fire. Not deliberately, but the effect was the same and Julie looked puzzled and slightly offended.

At the office, he was a liability in the smallest of talk. He was once in the lift with Valerie from Accounting when he inquired how her weekend had gone.

"Oh good thanks," she replied. "Busy. Saw my mum - lots of DIY."

Peter checked the lift's progress on the screen and thought about what to say, knowing he couldn't relate to her experience before settling on, "Right. See, I don't have that lifestyle."

"No," said Valerie. Peter saw her expression change before she answered.

Julie looked up from her drink. "I do a bit of everything."

Possibly freelance, he thought.

A man motioned to the empty seat next to Peter and he nodded. When he started to pull it away Peter shook his head to refuse him. "It's taken, I mean."

The man tutted impatiently and walked off in search of another chair.

"Independent? Freelance stuff?" Peter asked, anticipating that if she said yes his next question would be about computers, then probably Macs, then possibly about iTunes. He often wondered if everyone buffered their side of conversations like this.

"No, I work for Debenhams."

A lackey, thought Peter. *Dogsbody. Junior.* "Oh," he raised his voice in mock interest. Even with the Lana Turner curves, he wasn't attracted to her and he knew it was already mutual.

They took a sip of their drinks and Peter watched Jean Claude emerge from the back of the room.

"So," said Jean Claude. He held his hands out in front of him and looked at Peter and Julie. "We should eat." Julie smiled at him. "Will you join us?" he asked.

"I'm actually waiting for someone," she explained.

"Oh," he said, raising his eyebrows, "a date, maybe? That's-"

"-No, no. No." She smiled and looked embarrassed. "A friend from work. A girl I work with."

"At Debenhams," Peter told Jean Claude.

Julie gave Jean Claude a look of obliging, detached reluctance.

"Well perhaps you would both join us?" said Jean Claude.

"Oh," said Julie, "I'd like to, but it's just that my friend - she's, um, having a hard time. It's personal - I probably shouldn't..."

"Well another time, perhaps," said Jean Claude.

"OK," she said hopefully and smiled.

"We're not going yet," he said, pointing to their full drinks. "If your friend doesn't turn up or you both want to join us, you will say?"

"Thank you." She smiled at him again, took a sip of wine and watched the door.

Jean Claude sat down and raised his eyebrows at Peter, who laughed quietly and shook his head.

"Unbelievable," said Peter quietly.

Jean Claude took a drink, and then spoke. "Work. They are having the reshuffle when?"

"Starting probably three to four weeks away. But these things go on for a couple of months."

"And you've been there how long?"

"Fourteen years. There's also a strong indication that I can leave if I want."

"*REAL-ly*?" said Jean Claude, intrigued. "What did they say?"

"Karl said I should think about what I want to do."

"Interesting. He's making you an offer."

Peter took a drink. "What's severance, normally?" he asked. "About three weeks a year?"

"About three weeks," said Jean Claude.

"So that's nearly a year's worth of pay before tax."

"That's good, no?"

"Yeah," said Peter, sounding uncertain.

Julie's friend walked into the pub, moving quickly and looking defeated. They hugged and sat down next to each other. Julie shuffled them away from Peter and Jean Claude so they were out of earshot.

"So what are you going to do?" asked Jean Claude.

"I might take it."

"Of course you'll take it. I mean what are you going to do *after* you take it?"

"I'm not rushing into anything," said Peter, "I have responsibilities."

"To whom are these responsibilities?" Jean Claude was one of few people who used whom correctly and Peter found it reassuring. "To your team? Half of them may go. You have no family, no girlfriend..." Peter wondered if this was meant to make him feel better. "-which is good because you work too hard. It is good that you have no responsibilities."

"And why is that?" said Peter, humouring Jean Claude as he took a drink.

"Because you have no *dreams*."

"You should have bought that guitar. This is good - you should be getting this down."

"Ambition is the poison of chains," said Jean Claude.

"The *Poison* of *CHAINS*," said Peter. "- I love it."

Peter sang the words earnestly in a quiet, gravelly voice. Julie's friend looked over.

"This is very serious," said Jean Claude.

"Check it out, Tom Waits:" Peter lowered his voice for a second attempt while Jean Claude finished his drink. Peter interrupted himself "- OK. First of all, that doesn't make any sense."

There was no "second of all". Peter often did this.

"When you have responsibilities, that is when you wake up," said Jean Claude.

"It's funny, because I see your lips moving, but I'm hearing Eric Cantona."

Jean Claude was enthused, hopeful for his friend, which is what Peter needed to hear. Jean Claude's restlessness and passion had driven his own career at the expense of his family life.

"Maybe you're right," said Peter. "Maybe it's time to cash in the old pommes frites."

"I think so."

Julie and her friend stood up and sidled past Peter and Jean Claude's table, bags aloft and checking the place where they had been sitting as they left. Julie caught their eyes as she passed.

"Bye," said Peter.

Julie smiled and said to Jean Claude, "Bye. Nice meeting you."

"Enjoy your evening," he said in a kind tone.

He watched them walk out the door.

"How do you do it, man?" said Peter.

Jean Claude still smiling, raised his eyebrows at Peter, who said, "You spoke to her for like three fucking minutes, went for a piss and she's all-" he raised his voice a pitch- "'Nice meeting you, call me.'"

"She never said 'call me'."

"She didn't have to. You're like the French Jack Nicholson or something. And speaking of which? Worst. Wingman. Ever."

"But you weren't interested."

"But if I had been, JC?" he joked, "Hey? That's the issue here."

Jean Claude laughed.

"All right," said Peter, "I'll do it."

"You'll take redundancy?"

"What are the freelance gigs out there?"

"In this economy? With the time and money you have, there are opportunities. Also, you're thirty-nine, and that's a good age. Some years of experience, but not too old to still be writing and filing as a freelance."

"That's what I was thinking - doing some field work. Afghanistan is more of a story than I think we're hearing about."

"It is, yes, but you'll need to go further than the embedded press corps. The stories about the new schools and telephone projects - everyone does these. They are boring. And to see beyond that, you need experience."

"I have time."

"But you don't have reporting experience from hostile environments."

"I'll get it," said Peter. "I'll be careful."

"You'll be dead."

Peter laughed at the Star Wars reference but knew his friend was concerned. "Thanks mate. I appreciate your advice, you know that." He finished his pint in a long gulp.

"My pleasure," said Jean Claude.

Peter sought to deflect the heartfelt mood. He preferred sincerity to be implied rather than spelled out. He deflected the intimacy with dumb levity. "Ooh, you're like a little News Yoda, aren't you?"

Jean Claude looked away in mock disgust.

"Come now," said Peter, in the character's voice. "Drink you must, hmm?" He went to the bar.

Over a second and third pint they drew up a list of commissioning editors who would run stories filed by Peter from the field. It was a small handful of names, including Jean Claude's, but without knowing what the stories were it was impossible to guess the level of interest.

Peter felt a mixture of trepidation and excitement. After fourteen years on staff at a desk job with a salary, he was looking forward to the unknown.

"Looks like I'm going to be a reporter again," he said.

"Good man," said Jean Claude. "To News." He raised his glass and Peter clinked it.

"And all those who sail on her," said Peter.

"I don't understand."

"Don't spoil the moment, JC."

9
Thursday 15 July 2010
Hammersmith

Sarah watched Peter leave the newsdesk after the morning meeting. It was an unusual time for him to leave, and she noticed him not drift away but leave with purpose. He walked towards Karl's office and knock on his door. Karl said something to Peter without looking up and took some papers from his printer before walking out the door of the Editorial department.

#

Sally Van Der Kamp motioned for Peter to have a seat. Her demeanour had warmed to a thaw and Peter took this as a good sign. He thought it was a trait of someone who works in Human Resources that they have to be emotionally distant when they are dealing with complaints and mediating harassment claims or even telling people they no longer have a job. He reasoned this detachment would make it hard for them to show joy when the employee was happy with a company decision.

She looked contented and controlled, like a winning pool player before an easy last shot. A blank, hedgehog grin had fixed itself on her square jaw.

"So the company has considered your request for voluntary redundancy and I can confirm that in the reorganisation, your role will no longer exist and you will be entitled to a one-off discretionary payment."

"All right," said Peter in a tone of celebratory acceptance, one where the word "well" would not have sounded out of place beforehand.

"This is something you requested, and the terms of the agreement as well as its existence must remain completely confidential."

Not just confidential, he thought, but *completely confidential*. "That's absolutely fine," he said.

"We will confirm this in writing with timescales and remuneration," said Sally.

Soon and lots, thought Peter.

The meeting ended with few firm details apart from the fact that Peter was leaving NPL and he could start making plans to ride the fortune of his misfortune as far as it would take him.

Under the secrecy of the agreement, his colleagues would assume he had been pushed in the early stages of the reshuffle - "managed out" in corporate speak - and he would not be allowed to set the record straight if they did. He felt unsettled by this and he would have preferred to tell Jim. His sentimentality caught him off-guard, but he would miss him, even though they had not seen each other socially since a colleague's wedding.

Peter thought it might have been the sea air or the mixing of champagne cocktails and farmhouse cider that led to a drunken exchange in which Sarah had called him "lovely".

He had expected her to apologise the next day on the train back to London for being so forward, but she didn't, and on the journey home she recalled the rest of the evening in sharp detail. Nor did she mention it when Peter brought up the wedding celebrations over coffee the following week, so he guessed it wasn't a drunken compliment that she was happy to let stand.

He knew he would miss her. Since their recent talks and coffee breaks he found himself thinking of her in ways he hoped she was about him. In his imagination there were situations, innocent at first, an opportune risqué press or tug. Scenarios. Consequences. Results. And always her eyes, hazel and against more skin than he imagined he would know what to do with in controlled flusters of purpose.

As their recent hints grew more implied he became more attracted to her but he doubted she felt the same.

He put it to the back of his mind as he tried to stay focused on the job he knew he was leaving. Targets, audiences and traffic goals lost their importance and he kept up page impressions and the appearance that he would be around for another fourteen years.

Sarah worked late hosting a live online chat about parents who homeschool their children. The movement, backed by e-learning organisations happy to play to parents' distrust of the government, had gained ground in internet forums. It was the kind of issue where those opposed didn't feel strongly enough to speak up because their kids were in school, whereas those in favour of taking their children out of school were vocal in their opposition to the system.

After an hour of moderating a one sided debate, Sarah stayed behind in the empty office and checked Twitter for any updates from Peter, but he hadn't updated his feed for several days.

10
Friday 16 July 2010
Hammersmith

Karl waited until Peter had taken off his jacket before inviting him into his office and handing him an envelope. Peter read the short letter, printed on NPL paper and signed by Sally Van Der Kamp in handwriting with the A's written in a flourish of two strokes, like the A's produced by a typewriter.

Dear Peter,

Further to our discussion on 15 July 2010 I can confirm that your role of News Editor is being made redundant. In accordance with the notice terms of your employment contract, you will be required to work until 17 August.

The remuneration due to you will be £47,372 and will be paid with your final salary payment. The company will assist you in finding alternative employment as part of our award winning outplacement scheme and we would like to thank you for you service over the past fourteen years.

You are, of course, free to seek independent counsel and we would encourage you to do so. However, if you have any questions, please do not hesitate to contact either myself or Karl Howard.

Kind regards,

Sally Van Der Kamp

WATER RUNS SLOW THROUGH FLAT LAND

Peter thought about the phrase *award winning outplacement scheme* and how only the world of HR could have an award for how they treat people after terminating their employment.

Peter folded the letter and put it back in the envelope. He smiled at Karl, left his office, and walked up the stairs to the corporate department on the top floor.

The HR department was like a small office of its own – a company within a company, which had its own secretary behind a desk in a small reception area made up of a small table and two chairs. Two small rooms with frosted glass doors made up one side of the space – cubicles where candidates could be interviewed in privacy or fired candidly.

"Is Sally around please?" he asked the Australian secretary whose name he didn't know.

"I can check. Do you have an appointment to see her?"

"No, sorry."

"Can I take your name?"

"Peter Beckenham."

He thought her expression changed, but he couldn't be sure. A certain gravity, perhaps.

"I'll let her know you're here."

Peter nodded.

"If you'd like to have a seat," she said.

The secretary made a phone call in a low voice and Sally appeared as summoned.

"Peter," she said. "Hello."

She cocked her head slightly in a display of empathy that was cautious not to be apologetic.

"Hi Sally. Do you have five minutes?"

She looked at the envelope in his hand. "Of course," she said. "Let's go in here." She motioned towards one of the rooms with the frosted glass doors.

"Great." Peter opened the door and stood to the side to allow her to enter.

"Please," she said, and gestured for him to walk in first.

They took seats across from each other on opposite sides of a round table.

"Thanks for your time," said Peter.

"That's all right, of course. How can I help?"

"So Karl gave me your letter and I'm fine with it-"

"Good," she said. She smiled for the first time, feeling it was appropriate to do so.

"Since then, I've been thinking about my longer term future. I've been in online news for a long time and I think I understand the market pretty well, so I've decided to start my own business."

"Oh?"

"I want to do something in the same field, but on the content side as an independent agency, as a rival of the big agencies like Reuters or AP."

"Sounds exciting," said Sally.

"Now, I'm guessing that the terms of my redundancy state that I won't be able to work with or for NPL for a while."

"That's correct. For a period of 12 months after the date your role is made redundant."

"So," said Peter, "I'd be approaching other internet service providers. Our competitors."

"I see."

"*Your* competitors, I should say." He smiled and looked up and left towards the ceiling for a moment. "I'm going to have to get used to saying that," he said.

She smiled a second time.

"But if other companies use my services," he said, "it would threaten NPL."

"Right." Her intonation implied she wanted him to keep speaking.

"Well if these other companies use me as an agency to provide content, it'll threaten NPL as a news provider." He paused, but Sally said nothing. "The longer I'm here at the company, the more information I'm gathering about a business whose audience I would be targeting once I leave the company."

Sally thought for a moment. "Well we wouldn't advise you to talk to any competitors until you leave the company."

"And that's fine," said Peter, "and I accept that, but staying at NPL gives me a considerable advantage while I build my business ahead of talking to the, *your*, competitors."

"OK. Let me talk to Karl and get back to you. Is there anything else?"

"No. Thanks Sally."

"You're welcome."

He thought she gave him a congratulatory smile. One that said "Well played" perhaps, but he was tired with trying to read her thoughts and wanted to leave the room, the mini office on the other side of the frosted glass, and the building that had been his workplace since 1996.

HR had no choice but to let him leave immediately and he slipped out of the NPL unnoticed at 10:30. He sent Jim an email from his phone saying he needed to work from home and he spent the rest of the morning in the park around the corner from the office making a list of the equipment he would need to set himself up as a freelance journalist.

Sarah arrived at the office at eleven o'clock and looked for Peter on her way to the kitchen. As she passed the newsdesk she asked Jim if Peter had come into work yet.

"He was in earlier, but he's working from home for the rest of the day."

"Ok, thanks."

"Any reason? Anything I can help with?"

"No, it's fine," she said, looking at his desk. "Thanks though."

His desk had not been cleared, but it was unusually tidy, which did nothing to reassure her.

Just before lunch she received an email.

Date: 16 July, 2010. 12:29:15 GMT+1
From: Peter.Beckenham@corp.npl.com
To: Sarah.Copland@corp.npl.com
Subject: Are you free?
Message:

As above.

She replied.

Date: 16 July, 2010. 12:31:20 GMT+1
From: Sarah.Copland@corp.npl.com
To: Peter.Beckenham@corp.npl.com
Subject: RE: Are you free?
Message:

Can be. Where are you?

At around three o'clock her phone rang.

"Come for a coffee."

"What?"

"It's Peter."

"I know it's you. But right now?"

"I'm shipping out. Come for a coffee. You're paying."

"You're what?"

"'PAY-ing'"

"No, *you're* what. Shipping *out?*"

"Come downstairs."

"Where are you?"

"Downstairs. Come downstairs."

She took the lift down to the reception area and said hello, moving to touch his hand. He stepped close to her and she brushed his arm in a gesture more supportive than tender and one which she regretted instantly.

"This way," he said. He led her out of the building and they crossed the street.

"Where are you going?"

"Coffee."

"*Peter*," she said in admonishment.

"Afghanistan."

"You're going to Afghanistan for coffee?"

"*Sarah.*"

He held open the cafe door.

"Afghanistan?"

"I'll get these. Have a seat."

She sank into a chair and thought about all the questions she would have when he came back to the table. He knew she would ask him to reconsider, and her alarmed tone had already revealed her growing feelings for him, even more than the touch in reception which in the hindsight of her regret had seemed more like a lunge.

He returned with two coffees and put them down. "That's four sixty," he said.

She gave him a five pound note and he went back to the counter.

He returned with a variety of sugars.

"Afghanistan," she said.

"Yes."

"And why?"

"OK. Long story short. There's going to be a reshuffle."

The corner of Sarah's mouth twitched and she looked up and left to accept the information before she let out a sigh and her eyes returned to Peter. "Right," she said in a breathless, flat tone.

"And what with my tweet and stuff, I've been talking to Karl and have been offered a redundancy. But you don't know that."

"Starting when?" Sarah knew he would say Monday, but she asked the question anyway.

"Monday. I think News is going to be hit quite hard. I'm tired of defending my job, I've been here fourteen years, and I thought why not." He framed the question like a statement to gauge her reaction.

She answered more indignantly than she had intended. "So you're just *going*."

"Well, one door closes kind of thing?" He tried to sound hopeful but it came across as defensive.

"*Afghanistan*," she said.

"It's where the story is."

"Since when has that been an attraction?"

"It's fieldwork. I have the time. I have the money for once. I've got the contacts."

"But you don't have the experience. You've sat there, just like we all have, at the end of the wire, Peter. That's what you know. Newsfeeds and publishing. Audience numbers."

"But I've got the online skills. Half the hacks in the shit don't know the first thing about web journalism. It's all glossy bits to camera and flak jackets. That's not reporting. You know that."

"So what, you're just going to join the press pool out there like a seasoned reporter? All the big agencies already have people queuing up to be their man in Kabul."

"Those guys, they're embedded. Just another hack in the dust. They're earning a basic wage, eating free meals at the base, waiting for the next briefing or safe patrol. Do you know most of them never leave Kabul?"

"You're not seriously going to leave Kabul-"

"-and even if they do, what are they going to do up in the hills when they get there? They can't file video because they can't put it together without a team of four people, and the BBC isn't going to sign off that risk or expense."

"That's because it's dangerous."

"But because I don't work for a large operation and I'm not travelling with a group, I'm not a target."

"You're a target precisely *because* you're not part of a group."

"I wouldn't be noticed if I were out there as an independent journalist."

"And how are you going to get a story without being noticed? You haven't reported from the field in fourteen years," Sarah said.

"The stories aren't in the bases. The stories you don't hear about are in the hills."

Sarah grew annoyed. In the background a cappuccino was being created. It slobbered and roared to life.

"What's the name of these hills?"

"I don't know, just some *hills*."

She shook her head and looked away.

"The Hills of Stories," Peter said dramatically.

Her look softened. He could always make her laugh. He reached for her hand. She flinched, and was surprised to find herself wrapping her fingers around his.

"Come with me," he said.

She looked perplexed. "Excuse me?"

"Come with me to Kandahar. It's what we've always talked about. We can run away - we can go *tomorrow*. Oh Sarah, do please. Oh *do*."

He let go of her hand as she stifled a small laugh. She knew there was nothing she could say to dissuade him.

"When are you going?" she asked

"In about three weeks. Mid-August at the latest. First to Dubai for a stopover to see Jean Claude at Al Jazeera, then on to Kabul. I'm lining up some work for their website."

"You're going to do this, aren't you?"

"I have to do it while I still have a profile," he said. "In ten months' time I'll be the guy who used to sit down the end of a wire at NPL. Right now I'm the guy who is bringing web journalism to the front line. That's a product."

He shrugged apologetically and they both thought of where next to turn the conversation. He drank his coffee and struggled with how to change the subject. He asked her the question that had been eating away at him.

"Sarah, do we feel the same way about each other? Because I'm kind of hoping we do."

"I'm glad you finally noticed."

There was a stillness between them, one filled with nothing more than a breath.

Peter spoke first. "Well, isn't this a thing?"

"It could be."

"Right," Peter said, "I don't know if I want the whole girlfriend thing. I mean I do, but I don't."

"Explain, please?"

"The whole 'have a good day at work', 'bye honey', '*love you*'. That stuff." He hammed up a shudder.

"It sounds a bit nice," she said.

"It probably is, but it's not for me."

"You might change."

"I doubt it," said Peter. "People don't change."

"They don't?"

"No," he said, "*Life* changes. People adapt."

"Life changes."

"Yes. People adapt."

"I'll try to remember that."

He paused and looked at her. "Well, I should get you back for now at least."

"OK," she said as they stood up. She raised the inflection of the second syllable, inviting him to say more.

He walked her down a side street on the way back to the office where he knew they wouldn't be seen by any colleagues. She didn't question the detour and he took his cue from that.

"What time do you get off?" he asked.

"Depends." She said it like a suggestion, and she looked back at him timidly, as if the word had used up her confidence and she looked to him to replace it.

He leaned in towards her and she tilted her head as she inhaled, her chest rising and remaining there in anticipation. Peter found he had placed his hand around the small of her back. He pulled himself towards her and they kissed softly.

Her tongue found his top of his lip with a passion he hadn't expected from her. He opened his mouth and she released her breath through her nose as she dropped her shoulder. She lowered her arm and he felt the inside of her wrist braced against him as she reeled slightly while the unknown turned to possibility.

They broke away on a promise to meet after work and Peter went back to his apartment to take a shower. He thought back to their kiss and was caught off-guard by his emotions. He was worried about spoiling a friendship, but was struck by the feelings he had for her. It surprised him how much he looked forward to seeing her later that evening. He felt like he needed to - not just physically, but to share the time he had left.

He felt lighter when he met her around the corner from the office at six o'clock. He wondered if he was dressed too smart in his jacket and shirt, or if he should have booked a table somewhere closer into town, or if it was too presumptuous to suggest a restaurant near her house. He didn't want to leave her to suggest somewhere closer to his apartment because it wasn't very clean. He wondered why very clean mattered to him.

It was because of her. All the feelings were down to Sarah. He wanted to blame her for his doubts about leaving. He hoped anger would clear his conscience and allow him to slip away to Afghanistan with no strings attached.

After a light, almost ceremonial meal they went back to her flat where they made love intently, with a lust which started as purposeful and developed into a ritualistic appreciation as he watched over her, noticing the green in her eyes and her soft mouth.

She pulled her head into the skin between his neck and shoulder, her hands pulling on his upper back as he moved. She spoke before he came, her stifled mid-Atlantic swearing and groans becoming clearer when she said his name just once.

He held himself deep inside her until she opened her eyes that brought him into focus as she craned her neck up towards him.

For a moment he was happy to leave her wanting to be kissed, for the desire to fade to tenderness and mingle with the image of her beneath him for him to remember.

"Kiss me," she said. She lifted her head and said it again, repeated it like a demand. "For fuck's sake kiss me."

He lowered himself down and lay next to her as he let the tightness drain from his body as he kissed her gently.

She smiled and looked at him. He loved hearing her swear. It was a slutty librarian thrill that he could listen to all day, knowing that part of the appeal was that he would seldom ever hear it.

"Who's got a little nasty mouth on them, then?" he said.

She grinned and rolled on to her side to face him. She put her leg over his and he held it on his thigh.

"Miss Copland, I had no idea."

"Hmmm...?" she said, pressing herself warm against him.

Shit, she's beautiful, he thought. He hadn't noticed before how his stomach fell away when he looked at her. His eyes drifted over her breasts. He remembered his notion of leaving and the tightness returned to his chest.

She took a deep breath, like the one when they first kissed, which to him seemed to parenthesize the encounter.

"Do you want to stay?" she asked.

"Tonight?"

"OK."

Peter wondered if she meant generally.

She breathed again, this time an unresolved sigh.

11
Monday 19 July 2010
Hammersmith

His colleagues were told by email that Peter was leaving, and by the afternoon a few people had messaged him on Twitter. He didn't respond, but he posted routine tweets that illustrated everyday, non-work related activities.

Sarah watched his updates on the network, and she had posted just once, midmorning, on the Saturday before:

:(

Peter saw this and fell yet harder, the space between them half full and growing.

12
Thursday 22 July 2010
Hampstead, London

Peter started learning as much as he could about Afghanistan. Years spent watching the newswires had dulled him to events, leaving him not only detached but also ignorant. He had become a consummate skim reader with knowledge to match, and knew a small amount about a wide variety of subjects.

He knew what kind of government Portugal had, for example, but not the name of its head of state, or even the title of that head of state. *Prime Minister? President? Chancellor?*

He knew the name of England's rugby coach and the team's strengths. He couldn't name the head of the coalition forces in Afghanistan, or say how long it took to fly there.

For the first time in years he set foot in a library, and he found it a far more immersive experience than reading information on a screen. In the belly of the Gloucester Road library reading room he discovered a different Afghanistan - one of costumes and traditions rather than accounts of Improvised Explosive Devices and Islamic fundamentalism.

Peter felt the internet kept him connected to other people, but after leaving NPL he spent more time offline. He felt stewed in an anxious, offline loneliness while he resisted the urge to check his emails during the day, breaking a habit that had built up over years of desk-bound digital journalism.

His self-imposed exile did not extend to contact with Sarah. He thought their relationship had taken a strange path, from colleagues to friends to sex and finally a first date in Hampstead. He met her at the tube and they went to an Italian restaurant, where they shared a pizza and light conversation, and ordered a couple of glasses of wine and sat at two joining sides of a square table.

The waiter took their order and went to the bar. "You're really attractive. I don't think I've said that before," she said.

"No. No you haven't. Thank you. It sounds like a comeback now, but I think you are."

"Really?" She wanted to hear more and Peter was pleased to say it.

"Sarah."

"Hmm." Her eyes narrowed contently as she looked towards the back of the room.

"What?"

"You said 'Sarah'."

"Oh god. It is Sarah, isn't it? Have I got that wrong?"

"It's nice to hear you say my name."

Her expression softened to reveal an eager kindness. He loved the expressiveness of her eyes and her emotive subtlety. It wasn't something he had noticed from their time in the office, nor when they had sex. It was another facet upon which he fell hard and ricocheted onto the next angle of her personality.

"It was nice to hear you say mine the other day," he said.

She looked self-conscious. He wanted to reassure her. "You're beautiful."

"Do you think so?" she said.

"Oh my god. The *room* slows down when you walk in."

She pushed her leg towards him under the table and his hand found her knee.

After lunch they went to see Vicky Christina Barcelona at a small art house theatre.

"You realise this is a date," said Sarah as they emerged from the cinema, squinting in the daylight. "Oh, that's *right*. You don't want a girlfriend and you're unable to change."

"I didn't say that. I said *people* don't change," said Peter.

"I remember now. Well how are you adapting to our date?"

"Fine," he said. "You know it's actually a Woody Allen film."

"I know - you told me."

"No, I mean this is. We meet up on the street, we go to a movie in an upmarket liberal neighbourhood of a major metropolis, I'm in the middle of a pre-to-mid-life crisis. You're a little too well-scripted, but apart from that, we're in a Woody Allen film."

"Which makes you..." she said.

"Exactly. Diane Keaton."

She laughed and reached for his hand.

"I need to crack a few jokes about Nietzsche and run into my ex. Maybe a Sidney Bechet soundtrack and a kiss in a taxi."

"I'd like that."

"Really?"

"Mmmhmmm."

"I thought you hated jazz."

She smiled and walked closer to him. She squeezed his hand and stopped to kiss him in a way that to him felt soft and solemn.

He broke away from the kiss to pull her towards him as he stepped forward to hold her close in a protective solace. He knew leaving her would be difficult, and he knew he wouldn't stay. He wanted the pain to be all his.

He leaned back to kiss her head above the temple, to let her know he hadn't broken away from their embrace out of any reason other than to hug her and for Sarah, at least for now, to feel held; needed. Kept.

13
Monday 2 August 2010
Ealing

Date: 2 August, 2010. 12:19:23 GMT+1
From: ukpeterbeckenham@yahoo.co.uk
To: Karl.Howard@corp.npl.com
Subject: Plans
Message:

Hi Karl,

I wanted to let you know my plans before I head towards the light and attempt to find out if there's life after NPL. On 16 August I'm flying out to Afghanistan to take up the pointy end of journalism as a foreign correspondent (!?!?). Maybe I'm taking the phrase "time away" and "new challenge" too literally, but at least I'm safely avoiding the "new pastures" cliché.

I'll arrive in Kabul the next day and after a short stopover in Dubai to meet with former NPL big cheese Jean Claude Charbonneau. He runs Al Jazeera English out there and he's taking some pieces from me. He hooked me up with a translator who knows the ground. After some time in Kabul he's going to drive us to Helmand.

That's the game plan at the moment, anyway. Beyond that there are no firm plans, but I'll keep in touch. I also wanted to thank you for your support with everything.

All the best,

Peter

Peter was wary about adding anything more specific to his expression of appreciation at the end of the email. He wasn't sure if HR had facilitated his departure from NPL out of compassion or punishment, but he didn't want to take any chances in case the email would be read by anyone else in the company.

He was grateful to Karl, and he was pleased to see his name appear on his phone when it rang an hour later.

He answered. "Boss."

"It's a bit late for that now," said Karl.

"How are you? Nice to hear from you."

"Nice to hear from you, too."

"You got my email," said Peter.

"So, Afghanistan, eh?"

The question carried the same inflection as it did when Sarah had asked it three weeks earlier. For Peter the word had notes of adventure and romance, but for those he was leaving behind it was a question, or a challenge.

"And you're going independent?" asked Karl in the same tone.

"Kind of. I'm endorsed by Al Jazeera through Jean Claude, and they're picking up some stories but I'm on my own steam." Peter assumed Karl would know how much money he had received in his redundancy package. "He's hooked me up with a fixer out there. His name's Mika Hassan."

Foreign correspondents often used fixers - part translator, part guide, and a general trusted source on the ground. Fixers had essential local knowledge that covered everything from the number of a local dentist to where you could buy a stepladder at nine in the evening on a Sunday. "We'll be travelling together," said Peter. "I'll be in Kabul at first, then we're driving south to Helmand."

"Our boys are getting hammered out there," said Karl. "You should go embedded. Helmand's in the shit right now."

"Neither of us would pay an embedded freelance, would we?" he replied.

"Well listen, just look after yourself, OK? Send me Jean Claude's details. Does he have the translator's number?"

"Yes. They've worked together before."

"All right," said Karl. "Well just take care."
Peter thought Karl sounded worried for himself as much as he did for him. It was as if the concern was for his former employee was so great that it was contagious and had affected his own wellbeing. Despite being a journalist, Peter thought there were times when he really didn't understand how people's feelings worked.

14
Monday 16 August 2010
Dubai

"Multimedia," said Jean Claude in his heavy Gallic tone as he skewered an olive in his office on the fifteenth floor of the media complex that housed Al Jazeera's offices, "this is everything."

"Multimedia I can do," said Peter.

"Webcams, podcastings, tweets, skeeps -"

"I can do all of that."

Jean Claude continued. "- interviews, live onlines."

"-wait: *skeeps*?" asked Peter.

"Online telephone calling," said Jean Claude. "'ES'-'KAY'-'EE'-uh-'WHY'"

"Skype?"

"Skype, skeeps - you interview the Afghan people in their everyday lives and maybe we can use it."

"In Kabul?"

"No," said Jean Claude, looking disappointed, "People in Kabul, Peter, they do what? They make *business*, they sell *cars*, they work for *agencies*, they have restaurants. You must talk to the people outside the city."

"...the farmers, the doctors, the builders." Peter added. "I'm going to the hills."

"The *hills, yes*. And you film and you get the story you can not get in Kabul."

Only Jean Claude would have let Peter get this far.

He knew his former employee had little experience in the field but Jean Claude was willing to commission five pieces based on Peter's production expertise and knew he could file something back cheaply and quickly to meet the growing demand created by a twenty four hour news cycle.

Dedicated news channels originally intended to provide a snapshot of the world's headlines in 15 minute chunks, but the audience had other ideas. In the early days of CNN and Sky News, people sat down in front of their TVs to watch a few stories, and when the first story was repeated, they knew they were caught up with events.

Shortly after the dawn of rolling news television, people started receiving breaking news by text messages on their phones. In 1997 Peter issued the NPL News team with mobiles so they could be contactable in the event of a breaking story.

One of the journalists asked him if they would be able to check their email on it, something not possible on most phones of the time, and certainly not the ones within NPL's editorial budget.

"Well," said Peter, "you already have a PC at home, and you can access your inbox at your desk all day if you want. If you need to check your email between home and the office, you probably need your head examined."

Into the twenty-first century, email and web browsers were features of a new generation of smartphones and people started checking news websites on their handheld devices. Then Wi-Fi allowed them to look at websites on their laptops or on the move, and faster connections meant people were watching video bulletins on their mobiles and tablets.

Peter sometimes thought the world had changed to the point where everyone needed their head examined. In some ways he missed the days of "You give us fifteen minutes and we'll give you the world." Since then the audience had taken charge, and it was saying: "I have fifteen minutes, give me the world *now*. And I want to watch it on my phone. But let me define what I call the world. Actually, I have fourteen minutes. Go."

The demand for more news meant that editors like Jean Claude needed to produce a greater number of stories for the same amount of money. Peter was cheap and he would send back something different, in a media landscape where information the audience didn't know half an hour earlier had greater value than a single story that kept people generally well informed.

"Thanks for your help with this," Peter said to Jean Claude.

"It's work. Thank *you*. But I can't guarantee you'll get all the stories we need."

Peter took another sandwich from the low table between them. "I know what you're saying."

A smartly dressed European woman brought in a tray of baklava and coffee. She put it down and gestured to the empty plates on the table. "Would you like anything else or can I take these away for you?" she said, addressing them both.

Russian - or Eastern European, thought Peter.

"Thank you Natasha. I think we are OK." Jean Claude looked to Peter.

"Yes, all good, thank you." Peter smiled at her. She transferred the coffee and baklava to the table, refilled the tray with the plates from lunch and slid out of the room.

Peter turned back to Jean Claude who was admiring a different view, looking out of his window at the strip of new hotels and offices being built around them and taking root in the distance, wavering under an empty, baked sky.

"Do you ever land any way but feet first?" asked Peter.

"How do you mean?"

"Just - you. Sitting here in your glass tower with Natasha and your fucking ... tax-free olives."

"It's a matter of perspective."

"Really? Because I've tried looking at your life from a number of vantage points and as far as I can see it's all gravy."

Jean Claude stared at him blankly. Peter realized he had just described horizons of meat sauce. "It means everything works out for you," he explained.

"OK," said Jean Claude, leaning forward, "My family is in Paris and I am sitting in the middle of a desert. Do you think it would have been my choice, to have my free time in a pub with you in London-"

"- None taken," said Peter.

"- when I could be at home watching a film with my wife with my children under the same roof? It is better to be busy at work. I am not thinking about it, but in London? Free time when you are alone is not free."

Peter thought about this for a moment. He wondered if Jean Claude had consciously put his career first or if his wife had chosen to put their family above his ambitions. He knew that would have been fair, possibly even the right thing for her to do, but it would have been hell for Jean Claude.

"You still have a family," said Peter. "Your children love you. Your wife still supports you, through their best interests."

"And I accept this. I am free any time to go where I choose. To go back to Paris, maybe." Peter doubted it, but concurred with an optimistic pout. Jean Claude continued, "But you, you have a real freedom, a quality of the possible. I have to work and support the company and Celine. You have choices. I have-" his eyes wandered the walls for words - "...strategies."

Peter thought of Sarah and how close he had been to starting a serious relationship before he left. A nice thought, but with no regard to timing. It was planting bulbs in spring. He was relieved, as much for his own sake as hers, and yet it *was* a "thing" - they had come close to declaring it as such to each other, and they had asked themselves if that's what it had become.

"I'll tell you what I've got," said Peter. "I've got fourteen years in the belly of a soulless company."

"Which you left behind. That's a positive step."

"True."

"All of this is positive, Peter. You can't have doubts now."

"My only doubts are whether I can get you the right stories."

Natasha entered and took the empty baklava plate.

"You're an editor," said Jean Claude. "If you know they're good stories, they're good stories." He leaned back and smiled to punctuate the end of the meeting. It was a slow news day, which were often the busiest on the desk, as a lack of focus and consensus across the global media meant Jean Claude would struggle to settle on an agenda, since there was always the possibility that once the running order was decided, something bigger would break late in the day.

Peter didn't want to take up any more of Jean Claude's time, or squander his own. His flight was leaving the next day and he had a few final items to buy. He stood up and looked out over the spotless, gleaming rooftops of the resort complexes and shopping centres.

"Do you know where I could buy a camcorder in this shit hole?" he asked.

Jean Claude laughed and sketched out a map, complete with little palm trees. "Is there anything else you need?" he asked.

"Can I send a quick email?"

Jean Claude took him to the newsroom and logged him on to one of the computers.

Date: 16 August, 2010. 14:12:22 GMT+1
From: ukpeterbeckenham@yahoo.co.uk
To: Sarah.Copland@corp.npl.com
Subject: It's time to say Dubai (FaFAda-FaFAda)
Message:

Dear Sarah,

By the time this reaches you, I'll be sitting at a laptop on the 15th floor of the Al Jazeera offices, having just sent an email.

I hope you're OK, anyway. I just wanted to say hi and check in. Say hello to everyone there, even Jim.

Peter.

He returned to Jean Claude's office and knocked on the open door.

"I guess I'm all set."

Jean Claude stood and walked around his desk and gave him a warm handshake and reached out to touch Peter's shoulder as he did. "Be careful, OK?"

"Thanks."

"I have emailed you the numbers of our reporters and the translator. If you need anything on the ground, our guys have a lot of support there - diplomatic, medical, legal. Just in case."

"Thanks JC."

Jean Claude switched up the handshake to a hug and they parted.

15
Tuesday 17 August 2010
Kabul

There was a jolt of turbulence as Peter finished his Jack Daniel's. He looked for the flight attendant who had refreshed him in a mist of Ginger Ale as they started their descent. She appeared from the front of the plane as the crew made their final check that everyone was wearing their seatbelts before the landing.

Peter squinted through the window at the streets below, expecting to see signs of an occupying army but there was no sign of a military presence from any nation, just erratic pulses of traffic coursing between a mixture of new buildings, old walled compounds and clay brown housing.

The pilot lowered the landing gear and the wind resistance tugged the aircraft briefly before it steadied for the approach. After a smooth landing, Peter gathered his belongings and joined the slow march down the aisle towards the cabin door. He thanked the crew, walked down the steps and boarded a bus on the runway where he studied his fellow passengers. They were a mixture of businessmen, male and female aid workers, military contractors and a small delegation of Afghan women. Peter thought they could be politicians, judging by their age and cautious, charismatic demeanour.

The aid workers collected their duffle bags and

rucksacks in the baggage claim hall and the defence contractors picked up black holdalls that would have been marketed as having been constructed from "ballistic nylon" or "military-grade Cordura", instead of, simply, "canvas".

Peter hauled both of his hard shell cases off the conveyor belt and wheeled them behind him. He waved off a porter with his elbow and a frown while he made his way through the baggage claim area.

Jean Claude had arranged for his contact in Kabul to meet Peter at the airport. Peter had hired Mika Hassan, Egyptian, thirty-five years old and a Kabul resident as a guide for his journey into the further reaches beyond the capital into the provinces of Kabul and Kandahar before finally reaching Helmand.

Mika stood at the Arrivals gate of Kabul International Airport with a sign that said PETER BECKENHAM. In the five years he had lived in Afghanistan he had held a number of jobs in and around the capital as a guide and sometimes translator for a wide range of business travellers including mobile phone network contractors and doctors working for charities. He avoided working with any of the thousands of security advisers more out of regard for his own safety than as a matter of principal although he pretended it was a moral choice when his parents asked him about his assignments.

His father was the Egyptian Minister for Health and Population who had previously served as his government's ambassador to Canada and France.

A far-flung upbringing was not as wasted on Mika as it was on his mother, a former actress from Sweden who had overestimated the glamour of being married to a diplomat. She had a two-year affair early in their marriage with her Danish personal trainer, which was endured by her husband for the sake of appearances and his political aspirations. The liaison had ended by the time Emad Hassan was appointed to the Egyptian cabinet, but it ruined his chances of challenging Prime Minister Ahmed Nazif for the party leadership from where it was assumed he would make a run for the presidency against Hosni Mubarak.

Despite Astrid's infidelities, there was no doubt Mika was their son. He had a remarkable combination of his father's curls and matte complexion, paired with his mother's blue eyes and blonde hair. Mika's lack of political ambition was the result of an idleness contracted through a life of privilege. He had attended Royal St. George's College, a reputable private school in Toronto, where his father served his first diplomatic posting. There Mika showed an early gift for languages as he honed his French, adding another tongue to his already fluent English and Arabic and a smattering of Swedish.

Astrid was no psychologist, but she had read enough self-help books to know that Mika was "acting out" through his occasional problems at school. He once threw a teacher's car keys down a storm drain because he said that Mika, like most

Canadians in fact, was of "mixed origins". On another occasion, he called his third grade teacher a bastard, despite not knowing what the word meant.

But childhood rebellion soon turned to teenage apathy and his wanderlust bloomed as his father's withered. Emad Hassan repatriated Mika briefly to Egypt, a foreign homestead when he brought his family to Cairo and rejoined the ruling party that had supported him throughout his diplomatic career. In return it began grooming him for office, first at the Department of Internal Affairs, followed by the Department for Health and Population. Astrid remained in tow dutifully, but soon took up golf on the encouragement of Raoul, who caddied at Cairo's Orion Country Club.

In his late teens, Mika was duly dispatched to boarding school in Paris, where he indulged his interest in humanities and languages but achieved only average grades. He started university in Lyon but dropped out of his first year to travel around Pakistan and India where he reached the end of his money and his father's benevolence. Instead of returning to Egypt he took a job as a porter at the Mumbai Novotel for six months before moving to a position as receptionist of the Delhi Meridien where his fluent French was valued by the hotel management.

With no particular academic ambitions, he started learning Pashto and the odd phrase in Dari and in 2005, after two years in India he headed east, following in the speculative steps of businesses trying to get a foothold in Afghanistan. His first job was as a translator for the marketing manager of a company that sold fax machines.

Fax machines weren't selling in Toledo, but the Ohio firm, rather than diversify and develop new technology, found there was a market for them in the newly built state offices of Kabul.

The new Afghan administration wasn't drowning in red tape so much as riding a wave of new bureaucracy, and documents and policies were flinging their way around the new corridors of Asia's youngest democracy. Emails would have served the same purpose, but politicians the world over loved paper. "Your basic fax machine," stated the salesman from Toledo through Mika, "doesn't need technical support like a printer or a computer network."

The visit was a success. Soon after the Ohio office's reconnaissance mission, a flotilla of fax machines from the American Midwest stormed the government buildings and Toledo Man took an early retirement out by the lake.

Mika liked his part in the arrangement, feeling like a cog in the diplomatic machine without following too closely in his father's footsteps. He felt validated, involved in the rebirth of the nation that was growing both around and on him. As a former member of the globe's young diplomatic elite, he enjoyed the cosmopolitan atmosphere. Being in Kabul gave him the freedom he needed to balance his esteemed background as the son of an Egyptian cabinet minister and his trophy Swedish wife with the independence of being a freelance helper in an emerging market.

Peter recognised Mika across the arrivals area by his curly blond hair. He thought he looked like a Middle Eastern Harpo Marx.

"Mika. Peter Beckenham."

"Hello, Mr. Beckenham. Welcome to Kabul."

Mika led Peter to the car rental desks and they collected the keys for a CR-V, a compact, four-wheel drive Honda painted metallic blue. Peter tried to stop himself from forming early opinions about Afghan life based solely on the experience of the airport, but by force of journalistic habit he was keen to build a picture. He focused on similarities that magnified the differences.

The Hertz car rentals and American Express advertising could have been at any airport in the world, just like the tired businessman pulling a suitcase behind him while channelling a pained expression down a hands-free headset, holding a conversation while he rubbed his face with his free hand.

Mika took one of Peter's bags and they left the terminal. They walked into the dry heat towards the parking bays to collect their car.

"It's a little quiet right now in Kabul," said Mika as he drove to the middle of the city. It was 3pm, the markets had closed and the evening traffic was calm. There was dust everywhere, fine and light, and it attached itself to the new government buildings and their white stone courtyards, turning down their contrast against the brown baked bricks of the small traditional two story buildings. One neighbourhood on their route consisted of newly constructed compounds of two or three floor painted houses with walled and gated gardens.

"Who lives here?" asked Peter.

"These are the homes of local administrative and government officials."

"Where do the businessmen live?"

"Normally they live in apartment complexes and short term accommodation. Aid workers stay in guest houses, journalists usually stay in hotels."

Peter was booked into a two room suite in a small three star hotel called Residence Babylon.

At a crossroads he saw a group of six large American men in dark suits leave their chauffeur-driven car and enter an office building. Four of them were layered in thick muscle, the other two in fat. Dust conspired on the wind.

Afghan men in uniforms cradled guns on corners and outside the newer, fortified buildings.

"And the military?" asked Peter.

"They live in barracks on the bases. Private security staff live mainly in the government administrative zones."

Mika explained the different uniforms worn by the Afghan army, and the national and local police. Peter listened, repeating the colours back as his driver said them.

Mika braked suddenly when a man stepped into the newly laid road pulling a roped donkey behind him. A policeman stepped into the street, stopped the traffic in both directions and blew his whistle at the man, who took no notice.

"Who are you working for as a journalist?" asked Mika. He locked the doors and surveyed his surroundings while they were stationary.

"Myself, I'm doing some work for Al Jazeera. Jean Claude Charbonneau. I think you know him."

"Of course," said Mika, "Jean Claude at Al Jazeera."

Peter watched the man lead the donkey across the road and into an alleyway. The policeman waved them forward and they drove on. "- and I plan to do some filming when we get to Kandahar and Helmand," he said. "The plan is to spend the first week in Kabul, followed by three weeks in Kandahar in more remote Afghanistan before visiting smaller communities in Helmand."

He hoped the more rural areas would be the ones most affected by the war and whose contact with the West had been limited to the American and British armies. "Apart from that," he said, "I have few plans apart from staying with whatever story there is."

The man at the check in desk of the Residence Babylon announced proudly in English that the electricity was running, but the generator would not be fixed until the end of the week.

"How often does the electricity work?" Peter asked.

"If you need to charge a laptop it is best to do it now," said the man. "Some days we have no power for maybe three hours, but we have gas if you need hot food or water. We also have a Wi-Fi connection and the password is in your room. If you need anything, please, my name is Kamal." He gave Peter a key. "You are in Room four. Please enjoy your stay at Residence Babylon."

Peter thanked Kamal first, then Mika, who agreed to return the next morning with the car, which he would keep at his apartment while they were in Kabul. They said goodbye with a handshake and Peter went to find his room.

The hotel was originally a smaller structure built in the late 1970's before becoming emptied by war and pockmarked with gunfire. Its new owners had patched it up and extended it in a bold attempt to match the charm of a family run hotel. It was functional, however – two-storeys with twenty five rooms in a building shaped like the letter P. The eastern side overlooked a courtyard and the rooms at the furthest end overlooked a small but busy town square.

It had reopened four years earlier in the spring of 2006 after a spell as a boy's school. Under the Taliban, only boys were allowed an education, and as a structure it was more of a missed opportunity than a faded glory.

Peter took the stairs to the upper floor of the building. Room four was upstairs at the end of the hallway and had a blue door which had once been yellow. It was basic and functional, with a desk at the end of a double bed and a small chair next to a coffee table with a copy of National Geographic magazine.

He turned on CNN, fitted the adaptor to the plug of his UK four-socket extension lead and plugged in the chargers to his camera, camcorder, BlackBerry and laptop. He put the larger of his two cases on the bed and unpacked as far down as his towel. He stepped into the shower where the water thudded to a steady, soft stream.

He watched TV while he dried himself and he put on some fresh clothes. He opened the laptop and negotiated a Wi-Fi connection with the front desk and checked his email.

Date: 16 August, 2010. 16:05:08 GMT+1
From: Sarah.Copland@corp.npl.com
To: ukpeterbeckenham@yahoo.co.uk
Subject: Re: It's time to say Dubai (FaFAda-FaFAda)
Message:

Dear Peter,

Hi,

I hope you're OK. I just got your mail from Dubai and I'm thinking of you quite a lot, actually. Karl has been asking if I had heard from you, and that makes me a bit paranoid, but it's not as if we need to hide anything, since you don't work here and neither of us is in a relationship. Right? Anyway, I'm not sure what the internet access is like there, or when you'll get to read this, but I hope it finds you safe and well and being careful. Did you meet up with your translator? I hope you're OK.

Love,

Sarah

Sarah had worried about putting "Love" in the sign-off, but she thought she could dismiss it as protocol if he ever brought it up. Peter knew her formal syntax would give her license not only to use the word but to also set him up for a likeminded closer.

Peter thought briefly about the loaded "relationship" line but brushed his concerns off as jetlag and clicked Reply.

Date: 17 August, 2010. 16:55:08 GMT+1
From: ukpeterbeckenham@yahoo.co.uk
To: Sarah.Copland@corp.npl.com
Subject: Re: It's time to say Dubai (FaFAda-FaFAda)
Message:

Well, I'm in Afghanistan and it's amazing. I had no idea there were so many shades of brown. I know it's a cliché, but it's a place of contrasts. Some government offices look like hastily-built university blocks and then you have these low, two storey buildings made out of baked earth bricks.

I'm staying in the Sharhr-e-Naw neighbourhood, which is a mix of neo-colonial and post-ironica. It's pretty safe - there are lots of security forces around wearing different uniforms, most of them armed to the nines. The ones in the light blue pyjamas are local police, and even they carry machine guns. I've seen a US military convoy, but mostly there are businessesmen with private security in the area I'm in.

From what little I've seen, Kabul feels safe, apart from crossing the street, which is a death run. There's a points system that I don't understand yet, but everyone here plays it. Locals start on either a motorbike or a donkey and then progress through various levels. British journalists are double points and if you hit an American you lose a life. I'll get the hang of it.

Otherwise, apart from the western influences, it feels much like a regular Middle Eastern city but with a frontier town vibe to it. I can't tell if the bustle is lawlessness or a pioneering spirit, but I like it so far. I'll venture out tomorrow since I'm too knackered to get my bearings.

I'll sign off for now. I'm going to the markets and some government briefings tomorrow. As someone who hates shopping and politicians, life is starting to feel like work again.

I liked the sign off - don't think I don't pick up on these things.

I'm sorry we argued before in the cafe, but glad we made up after ;).

I really didn't think I'd miss you this much.

Peter

He finished unpacking, turned off the TV and tuned his radio into the BBC World Service. He lay on the bed and thumbed the pages of a Pashto phrasebook while listening to a feature about the September 11 attacks. The presenter prompted a panel of journalists who asked each other questions that were more interesting than their answers and Peter slipped into a three-hour nap.

He woke more refreshed than he would have hoped, considering it was just after 8pm. He walked down to the Babylon's restaurant, where people were eating together on two long tables, like sailors in the belly of a ship. The clientele was Western and looked like mid-level professionals and contractors from a variety of industries.

He was met at the doorway by Kamal the receptionist.

"Table for one?" Peter said holding up an index finger in the hope of defending his personal space.

"We eat together," said Kamal, who was also the dining room host. Peter stared at him blankly.

"Manger tout ensemble," Kamal said, not recognising Peter as the Englishman who had checked in a few hours earlier. He had misinterpreted his guest's underwhelmed look as one of confusion.

"We eat together? OK," said Peter with a tone of insincere novelty.

"Eat together," said Kamal encouragingly and motioning him towards the diners.

Peter sat on the end of a bench of the least full table, wishing he had brought a book or a notepad. He resigned himself to the likelihood of conversations about technical support, satellite phones, anti-Americanism, or the hunt for Bin Laden.

The topics came up one by one, and Peter brought up the question about the Al Qaeda leader. It wasn't picked up for conversation, and he thought it was being avoided by his companions within earshot - two young doctors, three administrative workers for the UN's World Health Organisation and a telecommunications engineer sitting opposite him.

After a more direct prompt about Bin Laden, the engineer spoke in a soft Irish accent, "It doesn't make any difference to me. I'm not fighting or reporting. Politics and your war on terror didn't bring me here."

"Well, it kind of did," said Peter. "You're a part of the reconstruction. We're the second wave of the invasion."

"How long have you been out here?" said the man.

"About seven hours."

The man smiled and put down a fork of pasta. "Colm Owen," he said, extending his hand.

Peter shook it. "Of the Killarney Owens?"

Colm looked puzzled. "Er, no."

"I don't actually know anyone from Killarney," said Peter. "It would have been cool to get that right. Peter Beckenham."

Peter ordered the chicken and bought a beer for Colm, an overweight man in his mid-forties, who explained that eight months earlier he had been living in London when British Telecom laid him off. This prompted him to go into business for himself installing phones in new offices.

"Best job I've had in years, if I'm honest with you," he said. "I set my own hours and I'm making way more than I would back in London." He watched Peter sawing at his chicken breast. He tore away a piece away and it skidded into the rice.

"And how are you getting work?" Peter said. "Through contacts? Do you advertise?"

"Not really, it's just word of mouth, you know? I get calls about the next couple of jobs before I finish the last one. Like I'm turning things down at the minute."

"Well I hope it's the same for freelance journalism," said Peter, staring into his food. He contemplated his next incision.

"I *thought* you were a journalist."

"How so?"

"Because you mentioned Bin Laden almost as soon as you sat down."

"This is Afghanistan, isn't it?"

"Most people see it as work."

"And that's it?" asked Peter.

"Pretty much," said Colm, "We're providing a service, we're developing the infrastructure - we're doing our jobs."

"Just in Kabul, though."

"Oh Jesus, yeah. You can work in Kandahar if you want. The money's better, but the situation there's a little shaky. Plus, you can't get the parts."

"The parts?"

"The materials. Wires, switches, tools. The suppliers are mostly around Kabul."

The war had kick-started a reconstruction which had created not only jobs in various services, but also the market to support them. "Wiring, cement, glass, tiles, telecoms and computer keyboards. Engineers and builders couldn't do their jobs without them."

"I guess that's where we're different," said Peter. "My job's a service and part of the war."

"Is the news a service?"

"For some. People learn about events and use the information."

Colm pulled an expression of emphatic compromise, a sign of friendly dissent.

"How much do people *use* a phone?" asked Peter.

"In Kabul, you mean?"

"No, I mean how much do people consider the actual physical function of using the phone as part of the conversation process? They just enjoy talking. Same with the news. It's information - it's the avoidance of being out of touch, or uninformed."

"People do business over the phone," said Colm. "They stay in touch with their families. But I can see how it's similar."

Peter didn't push the point, and the conversation turned towards the weather. After declining a second beer from Colm he retired to his room and slept through until morning.

16
Wednesday 18 August 2010
Kabul

Mika brought the Honda to the hotel at 10am as arranged. Peter had decided against driving anywhere by himself until he was more accustomed to his new surroundings.

He was due to interview the Minister for Education whose Grassroots Learning Programme seemed misnamed for a country with a landscape which from the plane had looked melted in smooth muddy tanned heaps, like a child's sand fortress after the first kiss of an incoming tide.

Mika parked in one of the spaces at the back of the hotel and they walked around the corner to the lively markets of Chicken Street. The street was previously known as Chahrahi Taurabaz until Kabul found its way on to the hippie trail in the late 1960's. The spirit of free love came via India and through Pakistan and it arrived in Afghanistan close to the end of a period of peace and prosperity, when laughter echoed off the tall, new buildings, the breeze moved bright silks, and the sun caught suitors' eyes which filled with hope and possibility.

A Marxist coup in 1978 sparked Russian interest after the president, Hafizulla Amin, turned out to be a psychopath. The Red Army tanks rolled into the country the next year, starting an occupation which lasted ten years and claimed a million Afghan lives.

The mujahideen, Islamic soldiers backed by US support, fought without fear of death and when the Russians withdrew in 1992, the Afghan fighters seized control and established an Islamic republic. Their victory was marred by the infighting of factions whose initial battles raged into the cities like a plague. Half of Kabul was destroyed and thousands were killed. In the mayhem the Taliban seized control, imposing its blend of militant Islamic oppression on a once prosperous and free nation. The organisation established a power base in Kandahar in 1994 and finally captured the capital two years later. Its extremism was barbarous - women were beaten for appearing uncovered, dissenters were executed, elections were a fantasy and the country descended into ruin and opium-funded global terrorism.

The history spoke uneasily to Peter, and it showed that although a proud country can fall into the wrong hands and be ruined, places like Chicken Street could emerge and revive an old spirit. Its market sold everything and nothing: mobile phone cases, carpets, spices, Steven Seagal DVDs, lamps, cooking utensils and batteries.

Peter talked to a man who owned a fabric shop. He was reluctant to be filmed, but gave some quotes about the new Afghanistan. Through Mika, he said he was hopeful that British and American tourists would soon come to visit Kabul and buy his products.

There was a warmth to the people and a hospitality among the older men, but few agreed to be filmed.

The opposite was true of the politicians, who loved being on camera but said little beyond a dry message of prosperity and autonomy for Afghanistan, and there was little Peter could sell as a story.

Peter and Mika left the street, returned to pick up the car and after being identified for accreditation, they entered the National Assembly building where a security guard searched them while their bags were x-rayed.

Minister for Education Ghulam Wardak met them in the Wolesi Jirga, the name of the lower house of the parliament, and the formal nature of the security gave the government building a note of aspiration.

"Education," the minister explained, "must not be overlooked in the investment in Afghanistan."

Peter agreed politely while he attached a microphone to the fine wool of the man's grey suit. He didn't want to respond with a question before the interview had started.

He asked the minister what he had for breakfast while he checked the sound levels and then adjusted the white balance on the camcorder that sat on a tripod fifteen feet away from the two chairs where they would sit.

The interview had been secured by Jean Claude, who had mailed Mr. Wardak's offices and provided Peter with the necessary Al Jazeera credentials, saying it was part of a series of pieces about the country's development as a player on the diplomatic world stage.

"All set, sir. When you're ready," said Peter.

"Excellent," said the minister, checking his watch.

"Are you happy to answer questions in English?" asked Peter, motioning to Mika. "I have a translator if you'd prefer."

The minister waved away the suggestion with an amiable pout.

"Right, then let's begin if you please," said Peter. He sometimes spoke that way to public officials. It was a guarded meter that allowed him to emphasise hard-hitting questions with a more colloquial tone if needed. He also became more English when talking to foreigners. The result in this case was a grand patois of pidgin bourgeoisie.

"If I may start with your views on how the country is adapting to the expectations of a changing Middle East," he said. He heard the words as they left him, a complex gibberish of Mr. Darcy meets Bond villain.

The minister looked at him and took a contemplative breath. "In the context of education?" he answered. He held his breath at the apex of an inhalation. His tone suggested an impatient nature.

"Yeah - um. Let's go from there." Peter raised a hand and looked at the running camera to establish an edit point. He turned back to the minister, coughed and paused, then smiled before resuming.

"Mr. Wardak, can you tell me how the country is adapting to the West's expectations of a new Afghanistan."

The minister replied with some stock phrases he

wanted to use, words he would have deployed regardless of the question. *Future. Investment. Understanding. Growth. Lessons. Development.*

As the interview continued, Peter knew he didn't have much of a story. When it ended the minister's assistant gave Peter the name of a headmistress of a local school which had just opened. She said he could interview her as long as he didn't report that the school had been built with funding from the US government.

"People will want to know the source of funding if the story is about development," said Peter.

"Afghanistan is a very proud country," she explained apologetically.

Peter took the headmistress's details out of politeness and a lack of other stories.

He edited the video of the Wardak interview late into the night back in his room and uploaded the file to Al Jazeera's servers, emailed Jean Claude and asked him to call the next morning.

Peter went to bed knowing it wasn't his finest piece of reporting, but he was pleased to be working and productive after weeks of making plans.

He woke the next morning to the sound of the faint pitch shift of a passing ambulance leading the chorus of traffic that drifted across the top of the lower floor of the building and across the courtyard to his half open window, where a breeze rattled softly on the blinds.

He was getting dressed when his BlackBerry rang.

"Peter! Hello."

"Jean Claude."

"How are you? How is Afghanistan?"

"Brown. A very, very dusty brown. I just had a shower and it was like washing a potato."

"And how's the Babylon?"

"Much the same. Thank you."

Jean Claude laughed. "Good, good. Look, I watched the video interview with Wardak."

It was the "look" that told Peter he was being let down.

"Yes," said Peter with a hint of regret.

"It's - it's... there's not a lot there."

"I know, the answers were pretty boring and I couldn't press him on anything other than education. I would have gathered more by interviewing the actual school kids."

"That could have worked."

"I'm trying to get something on the fighting but I don't think that's going to happen in Kabul unless I'm somewhere by chance when it kicks off."

"You won't get anything about security in Kabul unless you are embedded in the press corps and go to military liaison briefings."

"And you already have reporters there with nothing worth filing."

"We do," said Jean Claude. "You will have more when you go to Kandahar. When do you leave?"

"Tomorrow. Maybe Saturday."

"Oh," said Jean Claude optimistically.

"I'll keep looking around in the meantime and report back and I know you'll tell me if it's something you want."

"Of course."

"And I appreciate your honesty."

"Always," said Jean Claude. "How is Mika?"

"Great. Nice guy."

"He is."

"I gave him the day off today."

"Good. Well say hello from me. So how do you like being a reporter?"

"It's great. *Reporting*, you know? Being out in the field. Not stuck behind a desk in some air conditioned office."

Jean Claude didn't rise to the jibe.

"Up on the fifteenth floor somewhere," said Peter.

"I know what you are doing," said Jean Claude.

"Sorry," said Peter. He wasn't. He missed the office camaraderie.

Peter looked at the clock next to his bed. *08:45.* "What time is it there?" he asked

Jean Claude paused. "Eight fifteen."

"Jesus, what time do you get in each morning?"

"About seven forty five. I like to beat the heat. It will be forty two outside today.

"Still, that's fucking early," said Peter.

"But I go home at 5."

"And yet you call yourself a journalist."

"And your only commissioning editor, yes."

"Fair enough. I did get one lead on a story."

"Yes?"

"It's a piece on schools, but they don't want a foreign angle. They want to show the country building itself up without external influences."

"Who paid for the school?" said Jean Claude.

"Uncle Sam," said Peter. "It's funded by US development grants."

"Well, we can run it as a piece about investing in the future. We can talk about the US involvement with Afghan children learning English."

Neither of them seemed particularly enthused by the piece, but Jean Claude was eager to help his friend out by publishing his work and raising his profile as a reporter.

"You should go to Kajaki. Meet some contractors at the new dam and talk about the opportunities for foreign workers. And I'll give you the number of some press officers at Vodafone. They're installing high speed data lines in the area for internet access."

"But the electricity goes out three or four times a day."

"You are much too practical," said Jean Claude. "Have you gone to the Silk Road yet?"

The Silk Road was a bar renowned and frequented by the western media.

"No, but I've read up. They're trying to bring back the notion of the foreign correspondents' watering hole. Should I don a white suit and sip G&Ts while I listen to the cricket over the sound of someone's marriage breaking up?"

"You wanted to work in the field."

"I know," said Peter. "I appreciate the commissions, by the way. Sorry they aren't explosive. Can I say that over here?"

"See what you can get from the school trip, but honestly we have run these before. Kids learning English, life after the war, religious freedom, freedom *from* religion. You'll do better in Kandahar. Are you driving down?"

"Mika's driving."

"OK. Watch out on the road. And when you get to the city, avoid staying in one place longer than twenty minutes if you are in the street, and do not leave your car out of sight for more than five minutes. Use your common sense and limit your risks."

"Are there any other stories you think people will be looking for from Kabul?"

Jean Claude sighed a weak laughed. "There are so many journalists in Kabul that if I knew what I was missing I would have it already, if you see what I mean."

Peter understood. He knew he was in the wrong place at the wrong time.

He explored the town on foot alone, walking back to Chicken Street where he had lunch in a Lebanese restaurant before returning to the hotel to read about Kandahar tribal politics among the warlords of the surrounding regions. He hadn't logged on to Twitter or Facebook since he left the UK and he didn't miss it, but he was missing the office conversations and even the workplace politics. He headed out for a drink, leaving the hotel before dark.

The Silk Road was a clean, dimly lit bar within a nearby residential complex that housed contractors and private security advisors. After a quick security check at the gate, he entered the grounds and was stopped at a booth by the bar's entrance where the ex-military contractors and bodyguards were asked to check in their guns. Armed or not, everyone had to sign in.

Peter had expected the bar to be filled with unscrupulous and shady characters conducting deals worth millions, but he knew that even in Kabul such meetings happened in brightly lit offices over coffee and emails.

There were American influences scattered around the city. On the way to the bar, Peter saw a man in jeans getting out of a Lexus flanked by bodyguards. Years of conflict had ravaged the country back into what critics would generously categorise as the Developing World but in the more renovated and westernised districts of Kabul, you could buy a bag of Doritos on the street and walk down it whistling a Tom Petty tune and no one would bat an eyelid, so it wasn't beyond reason Peter had found a bar that looked like something out of a 1980's cop movie.

The Silk Road was a little piece of Iowa in the middle of Afghanistan. It looked distinctly American, with a burger menu on the wall and neon signs spelling out the names of beers they didn't sell. The effort reminded him of British pubs overseas, where the decor was conspicuously English and they served shepherd's pie and played Oasis.

Guitar riffs and smoke filled the air, and there was the snap of a break at a pool table. The room was three quarters full, with fewer than forty patrons. Bruce Springsteen's Hungry Heart faded out and was followed by Everlast by the Foo Fighters. The opening riff prompted two muscle-bound men in t-shirts to high five each other over a pitcher of beer.

Peter scanned the room for hacks. It was a derogatory word when used by others, but a term of endearment among themselves. Peter considered it their own N word.

He could tell the media people. They didn't carry the briefcases or leather holdalls clutched by businessmen, but they always had equipment with them, secured in padded bags with straps and clasps, nursing cameras and laptops. The journalists would furtively scan their mobiles while they talked among themselves, knowing it wouldn't be taken as rude or inattentive. They made an occasion of every new order of drinks that arrived at the table. They laughed in short, approving sneers and spoke in hushed condemnation, unlike security contractors who laughed in appreciative relief and spoke about things other than their work.

The businessmen in the bar held conversations with people who appeared to be either clients or colleagues. Some produced documents as evidence to back up the numbers in claims they had been making. They spoke in earnest tones and promised to deliver the results for their investors and make money for themselves.

There was a high school feel to it - cliques within subsets. Peter felt that if he walked over to a non-journalist crowd they would be civil and shuffle around, but would wonder what reason he had to join them.

Contrary to its name, The Silk Road was a destination, and everyone was there for a reason in the same way they didn't simply *happen* to be in Kabul. No pedestrians had come across the bar by chance and wandered in for a beer. Everyone's presence there had purpose, and their intent carried on into the drinking.

Peter walked up to the bar, backed with bottles of common booze in front of a mirror. He caught his tired reflection as the bartender appeared with raised eyebrows.

"What beers do you have on draught?" Peter asked.

"Table service sir, have a seat."

Pacific Northwest, possibly Seattle, thought Peter.

"Thank you," he said, looking behind him. "Over there OK?" He pointed to a table where three journalists were sitting around a bottle of red wine.

"Be right with you," said the bartender.

Peter walked over to the group.

"Mind if I join you?" He wondered how much of a

hack he looked. Dark blue trousers, light blue thick cotton short-sleeved shirt, dark brown three-button jacket, satchel bag. *Seventy per cent hack*, he thought. *Maybe seventy five. A drink would put it in the high eighties.* He felt like a cliché, but he was comfortable with it when they pulled out a chair for him.

They were English, all with the national press. Simon was from The Times, Greg worked at The Sun and Anna was with The Telegraph.

"Peter Beckenham, freelance web."

"Nice to meet you. Been here long?" he asked Simon.

Peter looked at his watch and was about to answer when he thought they probably meant Afghanistan rather than the bar. It would have been unusual for them to inquire when he arrived at The Silk Road, but Peter hadn't immediately considered this when he started formulating his answer.

"Oh, you mean Kabul," he said.

"Yes," said Simon.

"Sorry. Since Tuesday."

"Oh, same," said Greg.

"Good," said Peter, "I was beginning to feel like the only new guy."

"Oh. No, I mean I got back from the UK on Tuesday. I've been posted out here fucking ages. But it was my daughter's birthday at the weekend. Ex didn't want me there, but it's got to be done. You have kids?"

"No."

"Probably best. I've got two." He waved his glass at his two companions. "Four if you count this lot."

"For fuck's sake Greg," Anna smiled at Peter. "He's been here three years and he thinks he's Bruce fucking Chatwin."

"Wasn't he on the Tiswas?" asked Greg.

"That's Chris Tarrant," she said.

Greg shrugged at her. "Bit before my time."

"What brings you here?" asked Simon.

"I took a career break."

"From what?" asked Anna.

"From being an editor. I worked at NPL? I ran the newsdesk."

"They're more like producers, aren't they?" asked Simon.

"Producers, editors, commissioners," said Peter. "Largely everything but writing. I missed it, that part of journalism, so I thought why not create the story?"

The bartender approached the table and Peter ordered a beer. Without speaking, the man pointed an inquisitive finger at the empty bottle of wine. Simon glanced at his companions. Anna nodded as she lit a cigarette. "Go on then," said Simon. "One more."

"Have you done the government stuff yet?" asked Anna. Interviews with politicians were the easiest material for newly-arrived reporters.

"Those are the only real stories I have at the moment. I was in the Chicken Street market today but didn't really get anything."

"It's all politics though at the end of the day, isn't

it?" said Greg in a friendly display of consolation.

They spoke about senior people they knew in the News and they all tried to acknowledge familiar names by linking them to office life, and stories both breaking and personal. Anyone who couldn't place a name kept quiet so they didn't appear to be uninformed about editors other people might have known.

Simon asked what Peter's plan was.

"Well, I'm planning to be here for the rest of the week and then I'm going to Kandahar."

"Oh, ok," said Simon, "who are you with?"

"I'm freelance."

"I mean who are you going with? Embedded. US or UK forces?"

"Just me. I'm going out with a driver. Driver translator guy."

They looked back at him.

"What's his name?" asked Simon.

"Mika. Mika..."

"Mika Hassan?" he asked.

"That's him. Do you know him?"

"Who?" asked Anna.

"Mika Hassan," said Simon. "Youngish chap. Al Jazeera's man. His dad's a minister in the Egyptian government."

"I know," said Greg. "Nice guy."

"Seems to be," said Peter.

"Yeah, he's good," said Simon. "He's a fixer with Reuters, too."

"So you know Jean Claude Charbonneau," said Anna.

"Very well. We spoke earlier today. I'm filing some video pieces for him. How do you know him?"

"I used to work for Reuters in Dubai. We were tenants in the Al Jazeera building."

"If it's the one they're still in, I was there on Monday."

"Hmm," said Anna in a blank acceptance of a world she already knew was small.

The bartender brought a bottle of wine and a tall glass of beer and placed them on the table. Simon thanked him and topped up their glasses.

Anna stubbed out her cigarette, took her glass and leaned towards the table between her and Peter. "So, you're going to Kandahar at the end of the week."

"That's my plan," said Peter. "The end of the week being tomorrow."

"And you've been here *how long*?"

"Two whole days if you count this one. I know I don't have much field experience, but I'm playing it safe. I'm not embedded. I'm not with a major news outfit. I have a driver and a rental car and I'm not out with an agenda. I'm practically a tourist."

"Just as well you don't have kids," said Greg.

"You're drinking with a dead man, aren't you?" said Peter. He barely meant it, but dark wit took the better of him. Simon looked uncomfortable.

"Look," said Greg. "I don't want to make you feel bad - you clearly have a lot more experience in the business than we have."

"You really have a thing about your age, don't you?" said Anna.

He took a drink and carried on. "I'm just saying - out in the *field*? It's not Kabul. There's no Silk Road and tall frosty ones out there. There's dust, and there's the shit, and you don't really want to step in either."

Greg was starting to sound drunk. "I know you've got this innocent, nice guy thing going on," he said, "and that is probably going to help you land some news, but the Louis Theroux act will only carry you so far." He leaned back to punctuate his point to a close. "What kind of stories are you after?"

"I want to tell it from the point of view of the farmers, and the people in the fields and the hills," said Peter.

"What do you expect them to say?" asked Anna

"*I* don't know. You have to have a little faith, don't you? Maybe I've been on the wrong end of the wire for too long, but you can't tell me you always know what you're going to get - how things are going to work out. That was always the ride for me, and I missed it."

"Well if you're expecting the unexpected, you'll find it in Kandahar," said Anna, "but I think you should reconsider."

"OK, what's going on here in Kabul?" asked Peter for argument's sake.

"How do you mean?" asked Greg.

"I mean what's going on *here* that the world needs

to know about?"

"He's got a point," said Simon as he watched Greg drain his glass.

"Bollocks to his point," said Greg, "There are stories *here*." Greg motioned around the room, drunkenly conveying a wider environment. "There is a new government, there's construction, a new university, a centre for the arts."

"Great," said Peter, "it sounds like Cardiff."

"Cardiff is *nice*," said Greg.

"Yes," said Peter, looking around for the bartender, then back to Greg, "yes it is. But unless Catherine Jenkins is going to get her tits out, there isn't much of a story. And that's not very likely to happen, is it?"

Greg considered this and shrugged. "I don't know, it might help the war effort."

"I know that in a strange way you are showing concern for my wellbeing," said Peter, "but I've *been* an editor. I'm sorry to shit and piss on your jobs here, but it's all in the hills. There's nothing coming out of Kabul that anyone wants to read any more."

Simon and Anna watched Peter refill their glasses.

Greg stared at the table. "I wonder if we could get a comment from Charlotte Church."

17
Friday 20 August 2010
Kabul

Peter woke hung over and wondered if Anna had given him her number. He checked the contacts in his phone and tried to remember her last name. A place, he thought: Mansfield, Madison; Marwell. It didn't matter. He found her too conceited, not in an intriguing way, with a bitter and disdainful streak. The media business was full of them, people he could never imagine saying: "I don't know much about that, please tell me more."

The problem was, he thought, people who openly admit their ignorance and seek to fill it are more interesting people and made better writers, but in most cases the journalists who pretended they knew already everything were quickly awarded the more senior positions and became less involved in the actual process of newsgathering. To make money in news you had to stop writing it and start providing it. You had to supply it to companies like NPL after other people wrote it.

He scrolled through the names on his screen and pressed the call button.

"Mika. Peter. How are you?"

He looked out the window and the rooms over the courtyard with the dusty benches no one used. Three olive trees stood thin in sun, shadowing arrangements of sharp blue hyacinths.

"I'm fine, thank you," said Mika. "How are you?"

"Good. Bit of a head on me this morning. I found The Silk Road last night." A housekeeping attendant pushed a supermarket trolley full of crumpled towels across the space, smiling as she did. "I'm ready to go when you are. How soon can you get here?"

"In two hours, I think," said Mika.

"Great. We'll leave at lunch."

Peter called the front desk and told Kamal he was checking out. He packed the smaller of his two cases and took a folded canvas gym holdall out of the side pocket of the larger case. He filled the sports bag with his electrical equipment and personal documents.

He hadn't written to Sarah since Tuesday when he had mailed her his first impressions of Kabul and to let her know he was all right. He didn't want to worry her by saying he was going to Kandahar, so he resolved to send another one when he reached the city. He missed her, and he didn't want to give her more of a relationship to be apart from. He reasoned that if the feelings were mutual, mailing her would just make matters worse as they grew closer.

He called the Armani Hotel in Kandahar on Jean Claude's recommendation and booked a room for two weeks with a possible extension. The name conjured up what he was looking for - affordable with aspirations to the luxury of which he expected it to fall short while offering a level of basic comfort.

He emptied the closet and packed the rest of his belongings, including his smarter clothes into the larger suitcase that he took down to reception for them to store until his return. At the front desk he tipped Kamal $20 and headed back to his room up the fire escape steps. The door to his floor opened as he leaned in to push it. It had a stiff hinge, and expecting to put some force into it, Peter lunged forward and through the doorway.

"Steady now," said the voice of a man standing behind the door. "In a bit of a hurry there, Peter."

Colm Owen looked at Peter, whose hangover caught up with him as he steadied himself.

"Morning," he said.

"Jesus, you look like shite."

"That's the Silk Road on me."

"Well at least you don't hide behind your sauces."

It was a play on words not wasted on Peter, as his Irish accent made the *r* of "sources" conspicuously absent.

"I'm stealing that," said Peter.

"You can take the man out of Fleet Street."

Peter gave a singular chuckle with an involuntary short nasal puff. "I'm off for a bit," he said, "heading down the country to Kandahar."

"Right," said Colm with an understanding, which implied concern.

"We're driving. Are the roads OK?"

"By OK if you mean *are* there roads, then yes there are. It goes through Indian Country, though. Take a jack and your wits."

"Will do," said Peter. "How long is the drive?"

"It used to take two days right, but the US Army Engineers built a new road so it takes six or seven hours. Unless there are US patrols."

"What happens then?"

"You're not allowed to overtake military vehicles. Security rules. If they're sweeping for IEDs, it can take ten to twelve. Depends on your luck."

Colm was still holding the door. Peter wanted to get packed and thought Colm might be going to breakfast or work and he didn't want to hold him up.

"Well," said Peter, "I told front desk that I'd be gone two to three weeks so I checked out and have a bag in storage. See you when I'm back?"

"Definitely. This place is like the Hotel California."

"What, steeley knives?"

Colm laughed. "Be safe and good luck with the stories. I'll keep a look out." He made an imaginary headline with his hands. "'Peter Beckenham - world exclusive.'"

"Thanks, Colm. All the best."

Peter and Mika were on the road by twelve. Peter felt energised to be travelling light, away from check in desks and departure lounges.

The traffic was heavy as they left town. Despite the risks of crossing the road, the capital's pedestrians seemed to lack a self preservation instinct. Mika had to swerve or break half a dozen times before they reached the faster flowing road that led them out of town. The Hindu Kush Mountains were shrinking behind them and Mika drove south into the sun for three hours, making little conversation above Peter's Willie Nelson CD.

Peter thought how bizarre it was that a little over a month after he had been sitting at a desk in Hammersmith, the same seat where he had witnessed the events of September 11, he found himself on a road that had probably been used by those who planned the attacks.

He used to tell the less experienced journalists working for him that they experienced walks of life out of step with their own. "We move in worlds of which we are not a part," he explained.

Ten years earlier, Peter had met William Hague, then head of the Conservative Party and arch rivals of the Labour Government, at a political event.

"How very nice to meet you," said the Leader of the Opposition, Hague's words sounding like he had glazed them in a fake sincerity.

Peter returned the greeting, exchanged pleasantries and made his way past some people he was uninterested in knowing to find a waiter with a tray of sandwiches. He grabbed some food and walked through the doors of the private club into the Kensington dusk, stepped between a parked Bentley Continental and a Rolls Royce Corniche and crossed the road.

One minute he had been standing in the marble hall of a Pall Mall club and the next he was loitering in a back street off The Strand with a pilfered cheese roll and a cheap suit. He called his producer at the office to see how many people were in the chat room for the live event with the only man mounting a challenge to Tony Blair's place in Downing Street. The live online chat was the first event of its kind by a British politician.

They exchanged a few puns about the internet and politics and he ended the call. He began eating his sandwich and looked back across the street at the club he had just left. He didn't belong in the world beyond those heavy glass doors. He was an observer, there to record and report, hoping his equipment wouldn't fail and that the interviewee would get something spectacularly wrong and create a bigger story that would gain NPL more exposure as a news organisation and Peter respect as a journalist.

His pre-event nerves had killed his appetite and he looked up and down the pavement for somewhere to throw away his half-eaten sandwich. The streets were upmarket and security-conscious which meant there were no rubbish bins.

He wrapped the uneaten portion on his sandwich in a tissue, put it in his bag and returned to the club. He showed his press pass to the security guard, who opened the glass doors for him. The hostess caught his eye, smiled and looked past him to welcome some politicians and campaign managers gearing up for the election everyone assumed the Conservatives would lose.

The room fizzed with bon mots and encouragement. Blue uplighting danced with the bubbles drifting up champagne flutes to a symphony of marble and neon. Peter moved across to where his colleague had set up their laptops and he looked for Becca, the public relations woman.

Her voice carried the Australian nasal tones, with a blend of long Home County soft vowels. "William's just talking to Sandra from Comms, then he'd like to say a few words before we get started."

"OK, so you think he'll be about ten more minutes?" asked Peter, knowing they were due to start in five.

He was not surprised when she answered, "Probably fifteen, to be honest."

The room grew louder and twenty minutes passed before Becca signalled to a man who spoke to a woman who touched William Hague on the arm as she apologised to the people he had been talking with. She led him to Peter who introduced himself and the intern who would be typing the answers.

"And this is live, is it?" he asked.

"Yes," said Peter. He wasn't sure if Hague would object, so he added, "We'll have someone screening the questions, and we only broadcast the ones you choose to answer. They arrive real time but the audience only sees the questions you respond to. Nothing else gets published."

"Fine, OK."

Hague turned to Becca and raised his eyebrows. She turned and signalled to someone across the room, who said "shh…" and touched someone else's arm.

This went on like lit beacons across a landscape until the sound of voices faded to a dull murmur. Peter moved off to the side of the small stage.

Hague watched the process and he knew the room would fall silent, but he spoke just before it did, timing the words just right so that it looked like *he* had commanded the quiet. The trick impressed Peter.

"So..." he said, "...so can I say..."

Across the room, a man with a couple of drinks inside him was talking to two women at the bar. He didn't notice he was on his way to becoming the only person in the room talking who wasn't the Leader of the Opposition. Someone whistled, a woman yelled "Quiet!" and the aide waved his arms like he was making snow angels against an invisible wall.

"Can I just say-" Hague said and smiled. Jim took out a camera and one of the PR people put his hand on top as he raised it to take a picture. Peter noticed this and looked at the press officer for an explanation. "Not while he's holding a glass," said the man. "It doesn't look good."

"Can I just say thank you," said Hague, "to everyone for coming out tonight and to Sandra and the team for pulling this together so quickly."

Polite applause and a ripple of consent.

"Four days ago - " He paused and repeated the words even though no one was talking. Then he laughed, as if to respond to something funny that someone might have just said, as if to show he was having a good time. Peter observed the man's deliberate chuckle, a performance that he was enjoying himself, that William Hague was someone you could have a laugh with - a man of the people, right there in the champagne bar of a private club in Mayfair.

Man of the people, thought Peter, *talk to me, pal, I got half a cheese sandwich in my bag, I'll tell you some fucking jokes.*

"Four days ago," said Hague, "Tony Blair invited some questions to be sent to him by email and they were sifted through by his staff and spin doctors before he answered them on his website several hours later."

The crowd emitted quiet grumbles of discontent.

"Tonight, with NPL, we're going to be answering questions live as they come in from the audience. We're not going to doctor the answers or hide from the public. Tonight is all about honesty, integrity and embracing the future in a way which the Labour Government is afraid to do."

Hague hadn't lied, exactly. Labour *had* screened the questions that were put to Blair, and the questions to Hague *would* be live. However not all questions to Hague would be published, so the spontaneous nature of a live broadcast was implied but not altogether accurate. But he didn't mention that as he went on to say something about values and quality.

NPL had secured its webcast easily because it knew the Conservatives would use it as a chance to take a swipe at the Labour government. Peter knew he was being used, the way that people who work in the news use stories and sources to their own advantage. He understood that everyone in the media is a tool at someone's disposal.

Peter left Hague with their interviewer and he didn't speak to the politician again that evening. Hague lost the election for party leadership six months later but when the Conservatives eventually won the election years after, Prime Minister David Cameron appointed him Foreign Secretary, the UK's new face on the world stage, fielding questions tougher than any the NPL audience could have put to him.

By 2010, Peter was still moving in a world in which he didn't belong, driving south towards Kandahar with Mika Hassan, with the mountains to their left panning away as the landscape turned to green patches of farmland. Willie Nelson seemed to fit as another oddly-shaped piece in a haphazard puzzle, as absurd as the emergence of William Hague as Foreign Secretary, whose negotiations with America and Afghanistan had brokered the UK's presence in the country. Peter realised he owed Hague more than he had previously thought. The politician's diplomacy, failed or otherwise, had in part led him to this road between Kabul and Khandahar.

After driving for nearly three hours they joined a small column of slow moving cars behind a convoy of five US Humvees - off-road military vehicles that made their Honda look like a toy. The trucks were decked out in various guises, some with antennae, others with a gunner on the top, some carrying soldiers.

The non-military road users observed the rule Colm told him about that morning and everyone stayed behind the Humvees. Mika drove at forty miles per hour for the next eighty miles while the sun dipped to their right, slow and relieved, behind the western mountains as if lowering itself into a warm bath.

Worry
Why do I let myself worry?
Wonderin'
What in the world did I do?

The convoy turned off the road at Qalat in the Zabul Province at seven o'clock and the other civilian traffic filtered away by eight. As dusk approached, Peter and Mika found themselves still an hour and a half outside of Kandahar. They were driving fast, but were the only vehicle in sight.

"Are we going to push on?" asked Peter, wary of the fading light.

"I think it's best," said Mika. He watched the road ahead.

"So," said Peter. "Do you like working with journalists?"

"Compared to whom?" said Mika.

Another whom, thought Peter. Interesting.

"Compared to business people. People with real jobs," he said.

"Journalists have real jobs," said Mika, missing the joke. "Yes, I like journalists. You are happy when life is sad. You are-" he searched for the phrase - "you are singing in the lifeboats."

"We're also often sad when things are happy."

"Perhaps."

Mika leaned forward and looked up into the sky out of the front windscreen. A large plane flew high overhead, leaving a pink blaze of a vapour trail in the sunset.

"I guess I always wanted to be a journalist. Pathetic, isn't it?" Peter ducked to look up at the aircraft.

"Not really," said Mika.

"At university I didn't have posters of Che Guevara or fractal hippie patterns on my wall. I had pictures of Mark Twain and Ernest Hemingway," said Peter. "Although in my defense it was the one of Twain in the tennis skirt scratching his butt."

Mika laughed and the pedal steel guitar on the stereo played out the remnants of dusk while Peter checked over the equipment in the holdall at his feet. The battery life on his phone had a quarter of a charge left but his camera had full power. He put the phone back in a side pocket of the bag and hoped the camcorder in the suitcase in the back seat was charged.

Peter was blowing and cursing the dust off his

camera lens when he felt Mika slow the car down. He looked up to see four men standing in front of an old silver BMW several hundred yards ahead in the middle of the road. The men came into sharper view as they drove closer. One of them held an AK47 assault rifle, another a shotgun, one held what looked like a handgun and the smallest member of the group cradled a rocket launcher across his folded arms.

Mika's face was a mixture of apprehension and resignation.

"Americans?" said Peter hopefully.

"Not out here in these small numbers," said Mika.

Of course not out in these small numbers, Peter thought, damning his hope. *Of course not standing in front of their car on an open road. Of course not in the dusk, wearing civilian clothes. Of course not with a BMW.*

"Sarge, me and a few of the guys are going to watch the road about forty clicks south of the base at sundown. We'll take the Beemer." Dickhead.

Two of the men waved them down with their free hands while the man with the shotgun pointed his weapon in the air. The shorter one with the missile launcher took aim at their car as they approached, less than a hundred yards away, driving at ten miles an hour. Peter hated the small figure already.

He looked young, barely more than a boy, and Peter knew he was not going to shoot. This was a planned roadblock and if he were going to fire he would have done it already, or would be hiding behind a rock or a building before shooting at them.

Not that there were any hiding places by the road, he noticed, the US military had taken care of that in its design. He knew the boy with the rocket launcher would not have been in plain sight if he had any intentions of killing them.

"Fuck it," said Peter.

"Put your camera away before we get to them," said Mika as he slowed the car to a crawl.

Peter put the camera away in the holdall by his feet, took his phone out of the side pocket of the bag and put it in the back pocket of his jeans. He took out his compact camera, pointed it out the window and took a shot of the landscape and put it in the glove compartment, hoping that if anyone found it, the photograph would be a record of their location with a timestamp on the picture file. He felt a short moment of pride in this forethought before realising that the view out the window had been the same for the past three hours. He quickly transferred half his cash from his wallet and put it in the side pocket of his bag, which he threw over his shoulder into the back seat.

Mika forced a smile at the men who wore serious expressions. He waved as he pulled up in front of them and lowered the window. He leaned towards the open air and called ahead to them in a friendly tone.

The man with the AK47 walked around the back of the Honda. He wore aviator style sunglasses, a leather jacket and jeans. The man with the shotgun was dressed in a green military jacket of no particular national army. He approached the driver's side and lowered his head to Mika's window. He looked at Peter. "America," he said.

Peter shook his head. The man behind the car tried to open the boot. He emitted a string of consonants with the word "Français" in it. Shotgun man hissed something back dismissively.

"USA?" he said to Peter.

"No, no," said Peter in an urgent, helpful tone.

"Eh, USA?"

"UK." Peter patted his chest.

The man raised his chin at this and frowned. Mika remained silent, frozen by indecision.

The youngest man with the rocket launcher was barely in his teens. He stayed back, crouched on his heels by the BMW, his weapon flat on the ground in front of him. He looked on, turning occasionally to watch the road behind them for traffic coming from the other direction. The man next to him, the oldest, held his pistol at his side and observed the proceedings.

"United Kingdom," said Peter. He racked his brain for sign language that depicted his home country. "England."

The man frowned still. "USA."

"No. Not USA." Peter exaggerated mock disapproval, palms up, face slightly hurt in an appeal for reason. "British."

The man looked at him.

"Um. Great Britain," he said. Peter thought about reaching for his passport and reached towards the

holdall in the back seat. The man stiffened as his eyes
darted towards the bag and Peter brought his hands
back to his chest. "England." Peter waved at his own
face. "English."

"English?" said the man, with a tone of
comprehension. "London English."

"London English," Peter said, encouraged.

"Chelsea football!" said the man.

"Chelsea *football*," said Peter, "John Terry - " He
drew a complete blank on every other player on the
team. He could picture their faces, but his memory
was frozen in the moment. "John Terry," he said
again.

"Ah, John Terry," he repeated. The man with the
AK47 moved back to Peter's side of the car so that
there was a man either side of the Honda.

The man with the handgun walked forwards and
approached Mika's window. He was in his mid-forties
and wore traditional Afghan clothing. He was better
groomed than the others, with a cropped beard on a
stern but intelligent face. Binoculars dangled from a
strap around his neck.

"RAF Tornado," he said, joining the conversation
in an accent that was acute but enunciated and clear.

Peter hesitated at the name of the British bomber.

The man carried on. "Chinook?" he said. "Eh?"
He spat on the ground. "HMS *Fucking*?" he asked
aggressively.

Peter knew the message behind his interrogators'
superior knowledge of allied military hardware over

Premiership footballers. Ridiculous as it was, he was inclined to let HMS Fucking go unnoticed.

"I'm English," said Peter apologetically.

Mika said something quiet and kind while looking ahead and the man interrupted with a blast of controlled outrage before barking something at his companion with the shotgun, who stomped around to Peter's side of the car, opened the door and dragged him from his seat by the shoulder of his shirt.

Peter clambered to his feet and stood beside the car. The man's grip returned to his rifle and he took two steps back. He raised the gun to his shoulder and aimed it at Peter's chest.

The man with the handgun slammed the grip of the pistol on the roof of the car, shouted something and pointed the gun at Mika's head. Peter wondered if there was such a term as a "slow panic", but it was how he could best describe Mika opening the boot, with the lever next to the steering wheel.

The boy with the rocket launcher put the weapon on the ground next to him and stood in front of the car watching the scene unfold. He looked surprised and slightly lost, reluctant to ask for instructions but unsure of his role.

Peter's eyes flicked between Mika and the shotgun at his chest, and the man with the handgun spoke in urgent, clipped tones to his colleague with the AK47 who took the bags out of the car and unzipped them on the ground to explore the contents. He replied before closing them and putting them back in the

Honda.

Peter scanned the sky for aircraft and looked on the road ahead for other vehicles, but they were alone.

The man with the handgun said something to the man pointing the shotgun at Peter. He lowered the muzzle and walked past Peter towards the Honda. He shouted something sharply to Mika, who opened the door and stepped out. The man with the AK47 led Mika around the car and stood him next to Peter. The man with the shotgun began searching the car's front compartments. The man with the pistol joined his companion and told him where to look.

Peter and Mika remained standing by the open passenger side door. They were silent with their guard while the search was carried out. The rattling of CD cases and sunglasses drowned out the hope of Peter hearing an engine of a distant plane.

The man with the AK47 spoke to Mika quietly below the commotion. He sounded almost concerned. Peter thought his cadence carried advice.

"He says 'don't move'," Mika said to Peter.

"What do they want?" said Peter.

"Do you want me to ask him?"

"No." Peter looked at the two men searching the car. A pencil fell out of the driver's side onto the ground. The man with the pistol picked it up and threw it into the foot well. "Do you *want* to ask him?" said Peter.

"I think perhaps no," said Mika quietly.

Peter looked at the man with the AK47. *Softer than the others perhaps*, he thought.

"Tell him our names."

Mika did.

The man looked over Mika's shoulder towards the companion with the handgun and asked a question. The man responded with a tone of instruction. On receiving it, he slung his rifle over his shoulder by the strap and patted down Peter and Mika before saying something.

Mika translated. "Give him your phone."

The man with the handgun produced a plastic shopping bag from his pocket as he approached them. He spoke to Mika.

"Empty your pockets," said Mika. Peter put his passport, wallet and phone into the bag. Mika put in his phone and wallet.

He issued an order of some kind to Mika.

"They want us to go with them," he said.

"In their car, I'm guessing?" said Peter.

Mika asked the question and received a short answer.

"Yes."

"Lovely."

The man with the shotgun finished searching the Honda, sat in the driver's seat and started the engine. The man with the handgun spoke to the boy who picked up the rocket launcher, walked to the BMW and sat in the middle of the back seat with the weapon resting on the floor between his legs and the rocket pointed at the roof. Mika was told to sit to the boy's right and Peter was led around the car to the seat on his left. The man with the handgun sat in the front passenger seat. The man with the AK47 started the engine of the BMW and the two cars pulled away.

Night fell as they drove in the direction in which Peter and Mika had been heading. The headlight beams of the Honda behind them bounced into their passenger compartment, illuminating briefly the back of a head, or the glint of gun metal.

Peter wondered if satellites or air reconnaissance planes had seen them. He didn't know if the surveillance cameras would have picked up two men pointing rifles at civilians in the dusk. He had heard somewhere that the imaging from spy planes could read newsprint on a subject's magazine. He wondered if they needed specific targets to pick out such detail or if it were even true. He doubted that every inch of Afghan soil would be under surveillance and recorded for playback later if the need arose like shopping mall security cameras. He knew the chances were remote, even on a road of such strategic significance as the highway between Kabul and Kandahar.

He knew his abductors knew what they were doing. From making sure they didn't leave a pencil on the road to planning the operation for sunset when there would be less traffic, it all appeared to be well planned. The safety guidelines and common wisdom said that driving at sunset wasn't advised, but the US convoy, which had spoiled their plans to reach

Kandahar by nightfall, had delayed them. He thought their disappearance would take at least a couple of days to come to light, maybe three or four, and new travel security guidelines would be drawn up on freshly-printed maps. The advisory would be upgraded to a warning - in capital letters, possibly with graphics featuring exclamation marks in triangular road signs.

The man with the handgun used his phone twice and didn't communicate with the driver next to him. During the calls Peter looked at Mika in the bobbing staccato flashes from the headlights behind them, piercing through the otherwise blackness. Mika was staring at his feet, listening intently to one half of the phone conversation in the front seat.

They passed five cars travelling in the opposite direction but no military convoys. Peter thought that even if they did there was little they would have been able to do to draw attention to themselves without risking their lives. He guessed they had driven for twenty minutes before they turned left off the road that would have taken them to Kandahar. There were no roadblocks or villages between the place of their abduction and the turn off the well-surfaced asphalt onto a hard, bumpy road. It was a something he was sure his captors would have checked in the planning of their operation.

Peter tried to measure the time using the music on the car's radio, but his rising adrenaline distorted his perception and he lost track of the number of songs as he weighed up possible outcomes of their situation. He wasn't even sure if the Afghan songs were between three and four minutes long like their Western pop counterparts. He had tried to count verses and choruses but gave up and stared out of the window into the veil of darkness.

The road surface became more uneven after what felt like ten minutes. Without instruction from the leader, Peter felt them slow down and turn onto a softer surfaced road that twisted in a steady climb.

He tried to keep track of their route, and guessed they had turned left, southeast and away from the valley through which the highway ran, and were moving into the hills that had been off to the passenger side as they drove towards Kandahar.

After perhaps fifteen minutes of the dirt road surface they saw the lights of a dozen small, single storey houses. The buildings were made of large bricks and smoothed over with dark coloured clay, monochrome in the headlights. They were spaced out ten feet from each other with eight-foot walls between them that made up small courtyards. Animal smells wafted through the driver's open window as they passed through the village.

They made a right turn between two of the houses and climbed on a softer surface that led three hundred yards away from the other dwellings where they came to a stop outside a two storey house. The cars approached to no reception; no one came out of the houses, as Peter thought they might when a car pulled up at what he guessed was 10pm. Beyond the building and further into the hillside lay farmland which in the headlights looked terraced, cut into the slope in a series of horizontal platforms.

The driver turned off the engine and switched off the lights and the area was dark again. The leader spoke from the passenger seat.

"We must get out of the car," said Mika with a studied, calm voice. Peter opened his door and was taken through the dark by the man with the handgun who seemed more relaxed than before. The driver collected the assault rifle from the foot well and opened his door at the same time as Mika. Both gunmen ignored the boy with the rocket launcher and showed no concern about leaving the BMW unlocked as they took their captives to the doorway of the house.

The building was isolated from the rest of the village on which it looked down from its vantage point a short walk further up the ridge. As well as being bigger than the other homes, it appeared to Peter to be better constructed, with shutters and a hard, pack dirt driveway that went around the side of the house. The ground felt dry and the dust filled Peter's nostrils and settled in his parched throat. He could hear children shouting inside the building and women ordering them to keep quiet.

The man with the handgun opened the front door of the house and stood in the doorway, motioning for Mika and Peter to come. Their Honda pulled up behind them and was driven around the back of the house.

Peter tried to catch a glimpse of anything its headlights might illuminate, but they settled on little long enough to let him form a picture - a hill in the distance, then beams into the sky, dissipating into a blanket of pinpoint stars on the horizon. Swirls of earth floated up to fill the space as the car drove past. It turned the corner around the house and disappeared. The engine stopped and the driver appeared, carrying his shotgun. The man with the handgun said something to Mika, who told Peter to follow him. The two men with rifles and the boy stayed outside.

Peter and Mika were led into the house and stood in a hallway lit softly by a dim overhead light with a red paper shade. The property was well built and cared for. Shoes of several sizes were arranged near the door, family photos spanning generations hung in frames next to ornamental weavings on the wall and heavy scarlet fabric curtains covered the windows.

As they were ushered forwards he heard movement upstairs from the stairway to their left. They walked past two closed doors on either side of the corridor. They were led through a small kitchen and the man opened the door at its furthest wall.

He shook the pistol towards the doorway and Peter and Mika walked through. He said a phrase in a more relaxed tone before closing the door behind him, leaving them standing alone inside.

The room was fifteen feet by ten with windows six feet from the floor on each of the longest walls. Two large, well-worn sofas were arranged sideways to the door, with the one to the right pushed against the white wall, and an armchair faced them at the far end of the room. The sparse seating arrangement was crowded around a low, rectangular coffee table.

A television was in the near left corner on a small stand. It was an old set, pre-flat screen, a cathode ray box with no plug on the power cable. The room's only door was the one they had walked through, with a windowless, painted brick wall at the other end. There was no other furniture, no wardrobes or drawers, and no shelving on the walls. It didn't seem particularly inhospitable to Peter; it appeared thrown together as an impromptu guest room furthest from the living area of the house. There were bars on the window that looked more like a deterrent to ward off opportunistic thieves than security for holding captives.

The man's footsteps led away from behind the closed door. Peter heard a woman's voice calling in a tone used for children rather than spousal admonishment. He recognised the sound of the Honda engine starting out of view behind the high window. He heard its wheels crumple over soft ground as it was driven around the side of the house and parked within earshot. He heard someone open and close the back doors and lock the car.

He followed the sound with his head before his

eyes fell on Mika.

"He wants us to sit down," said Mika.

"Like 'sit *down*', or 'make yourselves comfortable'?" Peter sounded impatient.

Mika shrugged.

Peter walked to the end of the room and sat in the armchair facing the door. Mika sat on the couch against the wall to Peter's left.

"His name is Wahid," he said. "The man in charge, I think."

"Well perhaps you can introduce me."

Mika didn't understand the sarcasm and Peter felt a twinge of remorse. He would have been more comfortable had the bitter tone been understood and Mika had known he was being insulted, but the fixer's innocence reminded Peter that it was his fault that they were in this situation.

"So what happens now?" Peter said with a more deliberate kindness.

"How do you mean?"

"With *us*. Are Wahid and his goons going to come back with a camcorder and a machete or are we going to make video diaries for a year?"

"I hope neither. Insha'Allah"

If it is god's will. Peter understood the phrase but asked, "Say again?"

"It is in God's hands."

"Yours?"

"Not *my* hands. *God's* hands."

"But *your* god's hands?" Peter asked.

"Not gods. God. *A* god," said Mika. "One."

Peter heard the muffled thud of the house's front door closing at the end of the hallway.

"So," said Mika, "you mean is it *my* god?"

Peter nodded once slowly as a reply, blinking to patronise.

"He may be yours also," said Mika.

"I doubt it."

"There is perhaps one god with many names."

Peter heard footsteps in the kitchen outside the room. "I'm not a religious man," he said.

"I understand," said Mika.

"Must be yours then," said Peter. There was a knock at the door. "Hel-*lo*-o." Peter called out in a farcical normality. The word carried a dipped third syllable.

Wahid entered the room and closed the door behind him. He looked at them both as he took a few steps forward. He spoke to them in English.

"Gentlemen. You have been brought here against your will. I know this. You are Peter?"

"That's right."

"My name is Wahid," he said. "You are a journalist?"

"Yes. I want to tell both sides of this story about this war and the occupation. I chose not to travel with the British or US armies because I want the world to hear what you have to say."

"And what do I have to say?" said Wahid. His accent had traces of English, and a formal education.

Peter didn't think he was a farmer.

"I'm assuming-" Peter paused. "-you want the army to leave. You do not want our soldiers here."

"There are no soldiers here. There is no war in my village. I do not want war, but if war happens, I know there will always be war. This is man's will. Today, there is no war. Tomorrow? It is with god."

Peter was unsure what to say.

Wahid said to Mika. "Insha'Allah".

Mika nodded. Wahid turned and opened the door, looking back to speak. "There is no story for you here, Peter."

He left the room. Peter tried to take stock of the situation. He thought that although these were not soldiers, they were armed men in a country at war. They had taken captives hostage and yet they knocked when they entered the room, and they had sofas and spare living rooms and god and BMWs.

Fuck, he thought, *I'm in Guildford. I'm two Jaffa Cakes away from a written confession.*

He couldn't understand his predicament.

"Why are we in someone's house?" he said out loud, and not necessarily to Mika. "Shouldn't we be in some kind of godforsaken hell hole?"

"I do not think these men are killers," said Mika. "Zia, perhaps."

"Another friend of yours?"

"The driver of our rental car, the man with the shotgun. And the other man I think is Samir."

"Is there some fucking Facebook group I'm not

invited to?"

"The boy, the young one, looked scared when we were taken. He is Ali."

"And that wasn't a real rocket launcher," said Peter, "or at least not a working one. Wahid's a smart guy. He wouldn't have let the kids hold an RPG between his legs in the back of the car."

"His son, possibly."

"That's what I thought. You wouldn't pick someone that nervous to go on a kidnapping raid unless you were already very close to them. And you wouldn't give them a fucking rocket launcher."

He stood up and walked across the room and listened for noises outside the door. He could hear something in the kitchen. He moved back into the middle of the room and looked at the bars on both windows. He stood still. "This was a fishing trip," he said.

"I don't understand," said Mika.

"Wahid and his son."

"-Ali."

"*Right*." He had always been terrible with names. He tended not to use them to avoid the possible mortification of calling someone by the wrong name. Peter knew the difference between Mika and himself was that he wasn't interested in people. It was a handicap for a journalist, but his passion for facts and events carried him through. "This is a father and son fishing trip. Maybe the other two are brothers, I don't know. They all take a family trip down the road.

Mother makes some sandwiches, they pack the guns and they wait for a soft target, something non-military that won't be any trouble, like phone engineers, businessmen, or journalists and their fixers."

"But if they had weapons, don't they risk being shot at by the Americans?"

"For what? They're minding their own business."

"They had guns," said Mika.

"'Self defence.' And with the binoculars they must have seen us coming from at least two miles back. On a clear evening like that with our headlights on? They had plenty of time to get the guns from a hiding place by the road. They probably had fishing rods with them. The only time they were a target was when we were actually *being* kidnapped, and then they had a perfect view of the area."

"So what do they want with us, these men?" asked Mika.

"I don't know. But they don't fit the picture of your average terrorists. We'd be dead right now if their plan didn't involve us being alive in some way." Peter realised after he said it how stupid that made him sound. He smiled to himself at the thought of a jihadist, a self-proclaimed holy warrior, making a flask of coffee and saying goodbye to his wife in the morning before a busy day. "Plus terrorists don't tend to work from home. They're more commuters."

There was a knock on the door and Samir, the driver of the BMW, entered the room without his AK47, carrying a tray of mint tea, meat and flat bread.

Wahid stood in the doorway as Samir put the meal on the small low table between the sofas. Samir said something as he set it down, and then walked out past Wahid.

"Goat," said Mika.

"Yummy," said Peter sarcastically, looking at Wahid. "Then again, I've never been kidnapped, so there's a first time for everything."

"We are not killers, Mr. Beckenham," said Wahid. His use of Peter's last name told him he had inspected his passport and documents. "Do not insult me. I hope the BBC shows me more manners than you. Eat."

He left the room, closed the door and Mika picked up a piece of bread.

They started eating in silence. The door opened again and Samir put their bags inside the doorway and left the room. Peter checked his suitcase and holdall, rummaging through his repacked belongings to find that his passport and work equipment were missing, including his laptop, camera and camcorder. He knew they had been removed and he didn't ask Mika to examine the contents of his bag.

"You did not tell me you work for the BBC," said Mika.

"I don't," said Peter. "I did, briefly." As part of his job at NPL, Peter had worked for a year on a project with the BBC News website development team. He had added it as a separate entry on his CV so that it appeared as a secondment in order to boost his own profile. The only way anyone in Afghanistan could discover that would be by looking on his LinkedIn profile page, where he posted his professional experience for people in the news industry to see.

"I've been Googled," he said.

18
Friday 20 August 2010
Hammersmith

"Jim, do you have a second?"

Jim looked up over the top of his screen at Karl.

"Sure." He turned to a colleague. "Carla, we're just waiting for the video from the train crash to go with the pictures, then could you put these up as second lead? Simon Cowell can move down to Alsos." The Alsos were less prominent stories in the margin under the heading labelled *Also In The News*.

Carla had recently joined the team as an Assistant Editor, one of three new hires across the Editorial department made shortly after the round of redundancies in which Peter had made his exit. Carla glanced away from the twisted train carriages and smiled at Jim. "No problem," she said.

She was friendly and good-natured. Peter had interviewed her two months before he left as part of a recruitment drive that was frozen when the restructuring plans emerged. She would have been hired straight away had it not been for the proposed changes that led to fifteen of the fifty-five strong editorial team losing their jobs.

She had impressed him in the interview with her preference for radio above television news and because of her subediting experience on celebrity and lifestyle magazines.

After the interview, Peter took the lift with her

down to the ground floor. He asked her opinions about the people she had met at NPL.

"Everyone seems really nice. I really get the impression that everyone's working together and they enjoy being here."

"Yeah, that wears off after a couple of months," he said.

Carla wasn't sure if he was joking. Peter couldn't be certain either, but he was keen to let her know she had done well in the interview.

"I'm glad you got to meet Karl," he said. "He'll make the final decision, but of the five people we've seen, you're the only one who has met him."

"He seems really nice."

Peter hoped that she didn't think her overuse of the word *nice* would concern her on the way back to her office where she worked as a web editor for a travel book publisher. She was friendly but cautious with her words and he didn't want her to worry. In the reception area on the ground floor he encouraged her by saying he would be in touch soon and he asked her again about her notice period.

Peter believed that the people who were drawn to online news production out of a compassion for humanity had very little opportunity to express it in their jobs, because few online journalists actually wrote. The best they could do was talk to their friends, who rarely understood, or other journalists, most of whom were past caring.

Sarah watched Jim follow Karl into his office.

Through the glass partition she could see them standing while Karl spoke. Jim had his back to the rest of the department and Sarah saw him stand motionless, as if not reacting.

Her first thought was that it was a restructure announcement. Jim had become a sounding board for the Editorial Director in Peter's absence. But Karl's body language suggested a deliberate patience to the point of sympathy. If they had been discussing layoffs he would have been more gathered, deliberate - possibly rehearsed, both seated, probably on Karl's request.

They would have talked longer than the five minutes they spent in the office, she thought. Someone would have brought them coffee. After the meeting Jim wouldn't seem so tight lipped and determined to go to the kitchen and Karl would have looked more relieved when the discussion had finished and would not have carried the apparent weight of concern back to his desk.

This had to have been about someone else, or something outside the office that concerned them both. She knew it was Peter.

Sarah walked to Carla's desk, where she was increasing the brightness on a picture of a battered suitcase lying in a bush.

"Carla."

"Hi-" she hesitated.

"Sarah. From Learning."

"Yes - sorry. Hi."

"Could you ask Jim to give me a shout when he's back, please?"

"Absolutely."

She beamed a smile at Sarah, which she adjusted when she noticed the worry on her colleague's face.

Sarah went back to her desk and she watched Jim carry a mug from the kitchen back to News. He was about to sit down when Carla said something to him and looked at Sarah. Jim eyed his coffee with concern, and then sat down.

Date: 20 August 2010. 15:15:12 GMT+1
From: Sarah.MacDonald@corp.npl.com
To: UKPeterBeckenham@yahoo.co.uk
Subject: U OK?
Message:

Peter, sweetheart.

Are you OK? I know if you're not then you won't get this mail or call soon but I wanted you to know that I'm waiting to hear from you, and also that I think we are in love.

Sarah x

It was the first time she had used any real term of endearment. Previously she had called him *loser*, *cockmuffin* and *fucktard*. *Baby* once, but even that had felt odd.

Jim remained almost stoically at his desk for two hours before Sarah walked over to News. She approached to find him squinting at his screen, angled forward in a false concentration.

"Jim," said Sarah.

He turned his head, then snapped his eyes from the monitor to her. "Yes."

"Can we talk?"

"Certainly. Coffee?"

"No thank you." She gestured towards the meeting room at the far end of the editorial department. "Do you have a second now?" She turned and Jim followed.

They stood on opposite sides of the table in the small glass-walled room. "Terrible news about Peter," she said.

"Yes," said Jim. He looked relieved that she knew. "We're getting worried. Karl knew he was headed to Kandahar in the early evening their time and he checked with the hotel there to see if he had arrived, and neither they nor the hotel staff he left knows where he is. Peter would have had the sense not to travel at night.

"Do we know if he's alive?" Her voice trembled at the significance and possible finality of her words.

"No," said Jim, slightly dismissive and shocked, "No we don't. We're not there yet. I mean, I don't mean 'yet' like *that*. I mean we don't *know* that. All we know is that he's missing. He checked out of one hotel and didn't check into the next one. No drama but certainly a concern. He was crossing dangerous country and it's unlike him to not be in touch, so it's being treated as a disappearance. Who told you?"

"You did," she said. "Just now."

It was an old journalist's trick and Sarah was surprised at how easily Jim had been caught out.

Jim's expression took on a gravity and he lowered his voice. "We have to keep very quiet about this. Wherever Peter is, it won't help him if the world's shouting about it. It would raise attention. We know that high profile missing people become targets, so this absolutely can not be reported. Karl has already contacted the news agencies and I'll talk to the editors, but only the bureaux chiefs, not the correspondents. Everything needs to be verbal - no Facebook, no Twitter, no email."

Sarah flushed with regret. "I emailed Peter."

"What! *When*?"

"This afternoon. I told him I was worried."

Jim touched his forehead, looked up at the ceiling and back to her. "Well now you have a reason to be." He moved his hands onto the backrest of a chair to lean against it in a dramatic pose to steady himself for his dreadful contemplation.

"So this is *my* fault now? When were you planning on telling me, Jim? After you'd spoken to every editor in News?" Her voice was raised. "Or were you going to leave it a few more days of me not hearing from him, when you must have known I would have mailed him anyway."

"Have you been in touch with him since he left the country?"

"Yes," she said. "We grew very close and we were a-" she paused, considering her words, "I mean we *are* - we're close. We were talking."

"Well, I didn't know that."

168

Sarah's eyes welled up. "Fuck," she said. She ran her fingers through her hair and pinched her mouth between her thumb and forefinger.

Jim stood in silence, unsure of what to add. Sarah left the meeting room.

In the afternoon, Sarah told Karl about the email she had sent to Peter.

"I've spoken to the Foreign and Commonwealth Office," Karl said, "but this isn't an NPL issue, and there isn't going to be a corporate response because Peter's no longer an employee. I'm doing this as a friend rather than as Editorial Director."

"That's really kind of you," she said. She felt a pang of sympathy as this reminded her how alone Peter was, even before he left. She knew Peter rarely met with Karl socially, and for him to take this on said much about Peter's small social circle.

"If you get any news back from Peter," he said, "or get an email back from his account, let me know and I'll talk to the Foreign Office. They have been working with Yahoo and they can see that his inbox has not been accessed and no emails have been opened, including the one you sent."

Sarah took little hope from this. Karl anticipated her next question.

"No messages have been sent from his account, either. Yahoo says that email to him has slowed down to the usual Facebook updates and ticket alerts. It seems that people are taking our 'radio silence' advisory seriously, which is a good thing for Peter's public profile."

"But what is being done? I mean practically," she asked.

"The Foreign Secretary has been briefed on the situation and is being kept up to date with all developments."

"William Hague?" Sarah realised her question was rhetorical and was surprised she even asked it. She thought that if she had said it to Peter, he would have responded with dry wit. *Is there any other kind?* It made her smile briefly to think of him saying it.

"Yes," Karl replied, "and there's a chap from the Foreign Office coming to see me on Monday. In the meantime, if you hear anything back from either him or his fixer Mika Hassan, please let me know. Day or night, weekends, anything"

19
Saturday 21 August 2010
Zabul Province

Peter woke from his first night in captivity feeling surprisingly well rested. He wondered if he and Mika would be moved, because their lodgings seemed too close to the main highway to be remote and their captors' house did not seem evil enough. Nor did the men themselves, he thought, apart from Zia, who was unpredictable and quiet, like a shadow against a moving surface.

Peter remained lying down and Mika stirred and turned on the opposite couch against the wall, the springs under the cushions creaking beneath him. Another noise, softer, possibly of fabric being unbundled - came from the kitchen behind the closed door. Quiet voices conferred, led by the deliberate instructions of a man who spoke last, followed by a sudden silence.

The door burst open and slammed into the wall behind it. Peter moved to sit up and was pushed flat onto the couch, hitting the back of his head on the wooden frame of the couch's arm as he was forced into a horizontal position by the person kneeling against his torso. He did not fight back, but raised his head in recoil of the blow.

He saw figures, limbs and people - burst into the room like a current. Zia held Mika down on the other couch and he moved the translator's arms effortlessly to put him in handcuffs before sitting him up. Wahid lifted himself up off Peter's chest and bound his hands in front of him with two cable ties. Peter was raised to his feet and moved to sit next to Mika on the couch against the wall.

Samir crouched behind the sofa in front of them and opened a sports bag. Zia pulled a balaclava out of his pocket, pulled it over his head and went into the kitchen. He returned less human, a masked man holding a carving knife.

Wahid looked at Peter while he spoke to Samir, who was assembling a tripod. Zia put the knife on the table in front of the prisoners and Peter caught his eyes, gleaming with a dark joy from behind the black wool.

Zia straightened up and moved the unoccupied couch to the far end of the room and returned to pick up the knife. He stood in front of Peter and pointed it at Mika, who stiffened and turned his head away, as if in denial while his gaze stayed fixed on the blade.

Samir mounted the camcorder onto the tripod and Wahid spoke to the prisoners. "Today you will talk to the world. We intend to kill you if our requests are not met. You are powerful men, yes?"

Zia watched Wahid speak. It was clear to Peter that he did not understand what was being said.

"I - I don't know," said Peter.

"Is this the truth, Peter?" said Wahid, "The man from NPL? The man from the BBC?"

"I don't work there any more," said Peter. He was unsure if downplaying his credentials was the right thing to do under the circumstances. He added, "I know people who work there. For BBC News."

"And your friend," said Wahid, turning to Mika, "A son of privilege, am I correct? Your father is in the government of Egypt?"

Mika looked crestfallen and scared. Peter wondered if an elevated status would work in their favour or against them. As the son of a diplomat, any harm to Mika could have political consequences, which Peter knew Wahid would have considered. As a member of the media, Peter considered himself more expendable than Mika, whose captivity could cause a flurry of diplomatic concern.

Samir nodded at Wahid from behind the camera. Peter imagined the scene through the viewfinder of the camera as the events unfolded, detaching himself perhaps as a coping mechanism, picturing himself on the screen as a pathetic figure being watched by British officials who would ponder his fate as it swayed like the knife held by Zia, who moved into position at the side of the couch.

Wahid placed himself out of shot next to Samir by the camcorder.

"Tell me your full names. Say you are being held and you hope our demands are met so that you can go home."

Peter looked at Zia, who held the knife and stood with his feet apart in a menacing pose. There were no flags behind them, no banners, nothing he had seen in previous hostage videos to identify the captor's allegiance to any country or organisation.

"OK," said Peter, obligingly, "what are your demands? We can work with you."

Wahid stepped forward and leaned over the low table. He grabbed Peter's short brown hair at the scalp and pulled his head down on to his right shoulder and shouted at the top of his voice: "Our demands do not concern you, Mr. Beckenham! Your life is in our hands! If you want to live you will do exactly as I say!"

Peter winced at the loud, nasal voice.

Wahid kept Peter's head held to one side and instructed Zia, who stepped closer and pushed the blade of the knife against Peter's neck. Peter felt his skin resist and form around the blade, and his mind entered a frenzy of speculation about how sharp the steel might be and how much tension his flesh would bear against it, pressed above his jugular artery. Seconds stretched into moments – moments that seemed inevitable.

Wahid looked to Zia and issued a command, one he had to repeat before the metal was pulled away, slowly with the sadistic care of a villain setting a giant mousetrap in a cartoon.

Wahid released Peter's hair and Zia stood upright. Peter sank into the cushions, the sweat on his torso sucking the shirt to his back as his shallow breath simmered.

Wahid walked towards Samir at the camera. "Do you think you are ready now?" he asked Peter, almost thoughtfully.

Peter studied him with in a baffled hatred that settled to determination and thin anger. He wanted him to know he thought they were despicable, and to feel his desire for revenge despite their selfish mercy for sparing his life.

If a tabloid newspaper had reported the incident, he thought, it might have printed that he had "cheated death". But he had played no part in it. He hadn't escaped, outsmarted or hoodwinked his captors, or evaded any circumstances, nor had he steeled himself for his murder. He had simply waited -

not even for an end, because an end would involve him being conscious of a definite last moment – he had just waited to see if he would continue living to experience the blade being removed from his neck while his insides remained in place.

Peter looked to Mika, coughing lightly and composing himself in a fluster of a hard-won relief.

"Ready," said Peter through gritted teeth.

"Good," said Wahid. He spoke to Samir, who crouched to look through the camera's viewfinder in contemplation, then straightened up to look at Peter and nodded with a blank expression worn to veil his feelings of remorse. The colour had left his face.

"I am Peter Beckenham. I am a British freelance journalist and I am being held by captors who want their demands met so we can resolve this situation and return home."

Peter wanted to deliver a message longer than a couple of sentences, but he decided not to include a location, even Afghanistan, and thought it would be more cautious to leave that option to Wahid.

"Please comply with them..." he couldn't think of what else to say and he looked at Mika, not sure if he was in shot. Mika looked to Wahid standing next to Samir. Wahid pointed at him.

"In English?" Mika asked.

Wahid nodded, once and emphatically.

"My name is Mika Hassan. I am a translator and guide and we are..." Peter thought Mika was also thinking about the location while milling over the sense of revealing it, or perhaps wondering what he could add that hadn't already been said. "-being treated well and we hope to be released soon."

Wahid waved his hand above the camera and was careful not to speak until Samir said something.

"Thank you," said Wahid. He left the room.

Zia remained standing next to the couch while Samir packed up the equipment, didn't look at Peter and Mika while he compacted the tripod and put away the camera.

Samir put the gear back into the bag and took a key out of his pocket. He walked around the table towards Mika and unlocked the handcuffs. He looked at the cable ties that bound Peter's wrists. Zia spoke a short sentence. Samir looked uneasy as he left the room under his partner's glare.

Zia stepped forward and removed his balaclava. He held the knife handle in his fist with the blade pointing up and put the edge against the ties between Peter's wrists and began to saw at the plastic, pulling tighter as it gnawed at his skin.

Peter wouldn't give Zia the satisfaction of his wincing, and when the plastic was cut through he didn't rub his wrists to soothe his skin, though it appeared to him that Zia was expecting a reaction.

Peter thought that despite Zia being the muscle of the operation, he seemed to lack the authority to act on his psychopathic tendencies without orders from Wahid, but Peter was not about to bluff against the man's perceived sadism, which was so pronounced that he looked bored when he wasn't inflicting pain or fear.

Zia was the last of the captors to leave the room, and he did so silently, closing the door with a last look at Mika, who appeared exhausted and lost as they found themselves alone once more.

"Are you OK?" said Peter.

176

"Yes," said Mika. "Yes, I think so."

"Come on, let's move the couch back."

"The couch?"

"Yeah," said Peter, "Come on, we can't have it looking like this."

Mika looked at him.

Peter stood up. "Mika, I need your help."

Mika sat forward, and looked at Peter for approval, as if to check that sitting up had been the right thing to do.

Peter said, "We should move the couch back, and I can't do it on my own. Will you please help me?"

Mika stood and walked around the low table in a quiet stupor towards the couch at the end of the room.

"Now. You get that end," Peter pointed to the end by the far wall, "and I'll pull it to where it was."

Mika hunched forward against the couch, bracing himself to push it forwards. "OK?" he asked.

"That's it," said Peter. "Right. To me."

Mika pushed and Peter guided the chair so that it was directly opposite the couch where they had sat like shamed wretches two minutes before.

"That's about right," said Peter. He sniffed. "Does that look OK to you?"

They both had tears in their eyes, glazed in denial at their situation.

"Back a little," said Mika.

"Back a little?" said Peter. He looked at Mika - the sense of purpose was returning to his eyes. "OK," he continued, "To *you* this time."

Peter pushed the couch forward by half a foot. Without purpose, he thought, there is no hope, and that's not a life - whether you'd want to live it or not.

"OK," said Mika.

Mika adjusted the position of the couch to his left slightly as Peter pushed and inched it forward.

"All right?" asked Peter.

Mika eyed the two couches, lined up perfectly. "I think so," he said.

Peter looked at him while he surveyed their work. Mika lifted his head.

"We're OK," Peter said to him. He gave a smile, which Mika returned gratefully.

20
Saturday 21 August 2010
Gloucester Road, London

Sarah usually spoke to her mother in the States once a week to catch up on family news. There were rarely developments but always concerns from a woman who saw her role of matriarch as being more important than the happiness of her only daughter.

Sarah believed her mother harboured expectations for her daughter to be married by thirty, to own her own home, to live on the East Coast - New York if absolutely necessary but only if a suitor, and she called them *suitors*, presented the right opportunity - and on each of these points, imagined or otherwise, Sarah felt she had failed.

Her mother often asked whom she was dating and whether her future lay in the UK, or even in the media in general. As an editor and an Anglophile, Sarah could challenge her with an eloquence that would put her mother's language skills to shame.

She called her mother in the evening when it was mid-afternoon in the town of Madison, New Jersey, and before her mother had consumed the first of the several glasses of wine she drank each day. Alcohol always led her to relate everything Sarah told her to her brother's recent experiences, however loosely related.

"Hi Mom," she said.

"Sarah! Ron, it's Sarah!"

Her mother would answer the phone and announce the caller's identity to whoever was in the room with her, before shooing away any questions relating to the person who was on the end of the line.

Brenda Copland kept very few personal interactions to herself. If someone told a funny story, she would laugh to anyone within earshot as if the joke needed to be enjoyed as a group event. When a person told a story about a misfortune, she saw it as her business to turn to another listener and ask them if what they had heard was as awful as she thought it was.

"How are you?" asked Sarah. She heard her father say something in the background, followed by silence. "Hello?"

"I'm sorry sweetie, your father was saying something. How are you?"

"I'm all right. Are you guys OK?"

"We're all right, honey, don't worry about us. We were worried about *you*. We haven't heard from you in weeks."

"I emailed you two days ago and sent you a picture of the flat," she said.

"Yes, but it's not the same, is it?" said her mother.

"It's not the same, no."

"Are you sure you're OK?"

"Well, yes and no."

"Oh dear."

"I've met a man."

"Good."

"-I didn't need your approval just then, but OK-"

"*Uh oh.*" It was a patronising tone Brenda used. It suggested the anticipation of Sarah's temper, which it usually induced.

"Would you listen please, Mom?"

"I am, honey."

Sarah's patience was running in short supply and she didn't want to argue with her mother but it seemed almost inevitable. She knew she couldn't give her any specific details about Peter because of the advised secrecy around his kidnapping, but she wanted to share what she could.

"There's a man and we really like each other and he's away on business for a long time," she said.

"Well, how long are we talking about?"

"I'm not sure. It's an extended trip," said Sarah. "He's a journalist."

"-Oh sweetie..."

"The thing is that I think he'll be away for quite a while."

"Well if he likes you I expect he'll come back."

"Why?"

"To see you, of course."

"No, I mean why do you *expect* it?"

"Why would *I*?"

"You said you would expect it."

"Honey, it's not about what *I'd* like."

"But you're making this about you."

"No I'm not, we were talking about you and this - man."

Sarah didn't volunteer a name. She ran her fingers abruptly through her hair where it reached her neck.

"Mom, do you realise that when you give advice, you do it by telling people what you want?"

"No I don't."

"Yes you do. You say: 'I should imagine that they will come over at seven' instead of 'they will probably be over at seven'."

"What difference does it make?"

"It's selfish, Mom. You bring it back to you. I was talking about me."

"So how I talk is a problem now?"

"OK, you know what? Let's do this another time. I'll talk to you later and you can tell me more about what you expect."

"Honey, really..."

"Mom, I have to go."

"Talk to your father."

"I really have to go now."

"Please promise we'll talk soon."

"I'll call you later. OK? We'll talk later."

Sarah hung up.

21
Saturday 21 August 2010
Zabul Province

Peter paced while Mika sat on the armchair at the far end of the room and wondered if the morning's ordeal would be followed by lunch. The high windows offered a view of the sky from the vantage point of a standing person. Peter climbed onto the sofa against the wall to look out the south facing window on to the village below. He could occasionally hear voices or cowbells from the homes when the wind blew up the northern slope, although it rarely did against the prevailing downhill breeze. The panes were sealed closed against the frames beyond the bars. The glass muffled the outside noise but some sound pierced through - goat bells and shrill women's voices carrying over the dry air.

He knew they would by now be considered missing, with lapsed Al Jazeera deadlines and not checking into the Armani Hotel in Kandahar. He was sure that Karl and Jean Claude would have spoken.

He reasoned that Wahid would be aware that people were starting to grow concerned, which made his timing of the video ideal to raise the most attention. Peter wasn't sure many people would be worried about him, but sixteen years of journalism had seen him make hundreds of contacts across the industry, particularly given his long service history with NPL, a launch pad for the shifting sands of senior editorial careers.

He didn't feel particularly grateful to be alive, but he understood the reasons for having been left that way while the video made its way to whoever Wahid thought had the most influence, the greatest concern and the deepest pockets.

"They wouldn't have killed us," said Mika. He looked at Peter, craning his neck to the window for sounds from the valley.

Peter stepped down off the couch and started walking again. "Zia might have," he said.

"I don't think so."

Peter stopped. "Motherfucker had a *knife* to my throat."

Mika hesitated out of politeness, not wanting to brush over the incident.

"What did he say?" said Peter. "When he had the blade against me. What did Wahid say before Zia took it away?" He waited for an answer with intrigue while he paced diligently like he was in a courtroom drama.

"He said 'Don't cut him'."

Peter turned. "Wahid said that?"

"He did," said Mika.

"He said it twice."

"Yes," said Mika. "The second time was stronger. Zia, he is the vanjesel, I think."

"Yes. Yes h- wait, the what?"

Mika replied, "Vanjezel. Boiler Room, Fast And Furious, XXX."

"Vin *Diesel*," said Peter. "Yes. The muscle. The cowboy. He may be along for the ride, but the planning is all Wahid." The roots of his hair tingled as he recalled having his head pulled to the side. "He would have done it, too. Not them, but *him*? Zia? He's an animal. He didn't think this scheme up, but he's the hired gun and he's probably a killer. That's why he's not bringing our food in. He's protection for

Wahid, who couldn't pull off something like this without someone like him."

Peter knew Zia would kill them if he had to, and that their best survival tactic was to give Wahid enough reasons not to let him. Their fate rested on a video file on a hard drive somewhere and Peter could not muster a plan.

An hour passed, filled with reluctant silence, which was broken by a knock at the door. Samir opened it and put their luggage next to the couch. He left the room and returned with a tray that he put on the table. There were two plates of cold meats and flat bread.

Mika thanked him and Samir gave a soft smile, small and shy. Wahid stood beyond the doorway and entered after Samir left the room.

"You have your bags," he said, pointing at their belongings, "I have kept the telephones, passports, cameras and computers. The rest is here. I would like your email password."

Peter's Yahoo address was included in his online CV on his LinkedIn profile.

"Why do you need that?"

"I want to see if anyone has tried to contact you. You are a journalist - people will know you are missing."

"You have my phone and contact list."

"You have not received any calls." Wahid said, and waited for a reaction.

"Well, I'm not much of a talker," said Peter.

It was more likely he had received emails, but Peter had turned off the inbox on his BlackBerry to avoid the high data costs charged by the Afghan mobile networks.

Peter knew no one in Afghanistan apart from Mika, Colm the Irish phone engineer, some journalists at a bar whose contact details he didn't have and a man called Kamal on the front desk of the Residence Babylon. He cursed his antisocial nature.

"Maybe you have some emails," said Wahid.

"What are you looking for?" asked Peter.

"Someone who is missing you."

"A ransom, you mean?" said Peter. "Is this about troops in your country, or is it easier than that? This isn't political, is it? This thing with us."

Wahid stepped forward, sat down and looked at Mika, then Peter. "This is a - diplomatic situation," he said.

"Do you mean a financial situation?"

Wahid didn't reply.

"How long do you want to keep us here?" asked Mika in English.

Wahid turned to him, said something loudly in Pashto, admonishing at first, then impatient and by the fifth and final sentence shouting home a point. Mika looked panicked, his heart rate increasing and face red with frustration and the sudden return of fear and perspiration.

"Your email password," he said to Peter sharply. He shouted at the door, and Zia appeared holding a rifle. "Now," he insisted more calmly.

Peter paused while he considered giving a fake password and pretending the account had been suspended, locking him out.

Wahid said something else in Pashto while looking straight at Peter. Zia took a step forward through the doorway, held the shotgun at his hip and aimed it at Mika's head."

"Monkey tennis," said Peter.

Wahid replied. "Monkey tennis?"

"The o is a zero, the i is a 1, the e's are 3's. All one word." Peter remained calm, not out of defiance, but resignation, short of heroic, but with a quiet dignity.

"What is monkey tennis?"

"It's a joke. Alan Partridge."

"Does Alan Partridge work at the BBC?" asked Wahid. "Does he work at NPL?"

"No, it's just a joke. It's not important" Peter shook his head. "Monkey tennis. The password's monkey tennis. With the numbers for the i and e's."

Wahid stood up and walked towards the door. Zia pointed the gun at the floor and followed his boss, who turned back to face Mika and Peter as he left.

"I am not a terrorist. I am a business man," he said. "This morning. The video, this was necessary. I did not want it to be this way, but this is how it is."

"So what happens now?" asked Peter.

"This is an investment. We wait."

They left the room. Zia closed the door behind them.

Mika wiped away the sweat from his face as his breathing returned to normal.

"What did he say to you?" asked Peter. "When you asked how long he would keep us here."

"He said my life meant nothing. He said no one would come for me."

"I'm sorry," said Peter.

"It's not your fault," Mika replied.

"It kind of is."

22
Sunday 22 August 2010
Zabul Province

Peter woke up in his clothes with his face dimpled by the pattern of the sofa cushion's rough fabric. He rolled his shoulders to work out the stiffness of a night's work of performing variations on the foetal position. Mika, shorter than him, was stretched out in full on the couch opposite.

He replayed the previous day's events. Little in his life seemed to matter before the kidnapping. He wondered if Wahid's explosive temper was purely tactical, a prop like the boy's rocket launcher, or if he had meant what he said to Mika.

Peter knew these were not terrorists. If they were, he and Mika would be part of a bigger operation. They would be in a cell somewhere, not camped out in a guest room, sharing the family bathroom. If the kidnappers were part of a terrorist network, he reasoned, Wahid would have been more secretive about their fate. Peter thought Wahid was waiting, and they were on the hook, part of a larger fishing trip.

There was a knock at the door. Mika looked up from where he was lying. Wahid entered alone, holding a piece of paper.

"Who is Sarah?" he asked.

Peter felt an elated desolation. "She is someone I work with."

"And she is someone who loves you?" He smiled at Mika and turned back to Peter.

"No, I work with her. That's all"

"Well..." He gave Peter a printout of the email.

His eyes were drawn to the second line.

Date: 20 August, 2010. 15:15:12 GMT+1
From: Sarah.MacDonald@corp.npl.com

He read the email slowly and last words twice.

…also that I think we are in love.

Sarah x

Peter was stunned, although touched. He knew Wahid had his advantage and would use it to its fullest.

"Do you have a wife, Peter?"

Peter said nothing.

"Perhaps," said Wahid. "And maybe Sarah it is just the whore of NPL."

Actually, thought Peter, the whore of NPL worked in Travel. Judith - summer of '08. Twice.

"And Alan Partridge?" asked Wahid.

"Who?"

"You said his name yesterday after this monkey tennis. He is also a journalist?"

"No, he is made up. He's a character on TV," Peter explained.

"Yes," said Wahid. "I found his website. Why does he not email you?"

"He-" Peter wasn't prepared to explain the convincing online presence of Steve Coogan's comic creation. He sighed. "I don't know."

"We will see."

The afternoon passed; then the evening. The food was bland, the portions were adequate and the boredom deafening. Both Mika and Peter had chosen lifestyles that defied routine, where the task was dictated by changing events, and success came more from productivity than strategy. To Peter, a day of corporate brainstorms in meeting rooms was a slow death, and one which resembled the time that dragged itself across their captivity.

23
Monday 23 August 2010
Hammersmith

News about Peter's disappearance had started to work its way around the NPL office.

The assigned liaison official from the Foreign and Commonwealth Office was a man named Adam Lipscombe, a junior diplomat, barely out of his twenties in a suit no taxpayer would have complained about funding. Karl was grateful the Government had sent someone in person first thing on Monday morning, which he attributed to Peter's position in the media, although the man's flighty nature and hurried sympathy did nothing to assure Karl that the disappearance was being treated as a matter of national importance.

They sat at the table in Karl's office.

"Mr. Howard, I'll be honest with you," said Lipscombe.

"Good," said Karl.

"The Ministry of Defence has been informed of the situation and allied forces in the area are aware of Mr. Beckenham and Mr. Hassan's disappearance."

"OK."

"However it is extremely rare for the military to mount a specific Search and Rescue mission for non-military personnel."

"What if his whereabouts were known?" said Karl. We know they disappeared on the way to Kandahar."

Mr. Lipscombe shuffled in his seat. "This is an active theatre of war," he said, "and our troops' resources are not unlimited. Any additional operations which are not critical to the greater military objectives would need to be considered very carefully in the context of the bigger picture."

"So you're saying he wouldn't be rescued even if we knew where he was being held?" asked Karl.

"It's likely that his captors, if indeed he has been abducted, are armed. At the moment, intelligence and diplomacy are our most useful tools."

"But we don't know anything and we're not talking to anyone."

"Then we have some objectives."

"We have nothing. The terrorists have my friend, and we've got our thumbs up our arses. How are-"

"-Mr. Howard," Lipscombe interrupted, "we don't know if Mr. Beckenham has been kidnapped and there's no knowledge of the involvement of any terrorist organisation. In my experience of kidnappings, the perpetrators are in touch within forty-eight hours of the abduction. Any potential captors would have no advantage in keeping him without making demands."

"In your *experience*," Karl said. "No disrespect Mr. Lipscombe, but you're how old?"

"I'm thirty four."

Karl thought he looked younger and awkward under pressure.

"In *our* experience at the Foreign and Commonwealth Office," he said, "there is a benefit to studying the situation and responding accordingly. In the meantime, your enforced policy of not reporting the situation has been exactly the right thing to do."

Karl knew it was pointless arguing with the man. Even if he could persuade him, it would never get through to the Ministry of Defence, Whitehall, Downing Street or however far he could take his case for military intervention, and the publicity generated by lobbying the Government would put Peter at risk"

Karl felt he had no choice, and the best course of action was a dreadful wait.

"Have you heard anything from Yahoo?" he asked.

"Email communication to him is still at a minimum," said Lipscombe, "which is a good thing. We know about the mail from Sarah Copland, but too much concern from friends and colleagues would inflate the demands in the same way as widespread news coverage of the event, if we are talking about a hostage situation."

"And we don't know if we are," said Karl.

"Exactly," said Lipscombe.

"What about mobile communication. Has Peter made any calls?"

"The last call was made on the morning of Friday 20 August to Mika Hassan's mobile. Records show both phones were in Kabul at the time and it was a short conversation.

Karl shook his head. "How could he go missing on Afghanistan's busiest and most heavily patrolled road?"

"Mr. Howard, Afghanistan is a dangerous place. It's a haven for opportunistic crime. The Kabul-Kandahar road can be quiet and foreboding in places, particularly where it is under the control of the Afghan National Army."

Security had been compromised in the handover to local security forces. The Afghan soldiers were mentally tough, and many were fearless, but they were poorly disciplined and difficult to train. US Marines called them the Flip-Flop Army, on account of their lack of equipment but eagerness to fight.

"There are regular patrols and military convoys along the road and Mr. Beckenham and Mr. Hassan's possible captors would have been reluctant to travel for fear of being spotted."

"And yet they were taken in broad daylight," said Karl.

"We don't know if it was daylight or if he was taken," said Lipscombe.

"We can assume," said Karl, "that Peter would not have been travelling at night. This was his first time in Afghanistan. He's smart enough to know what he doesn't know, and he would have been aware of certain risks. We can also assume he has been kidnapped because his mobile is off and we know he didn't turn up at the hotel in Kandahar."

"Mr. Howard, we have to wait. It's a patrolled area, and if - *if* - he has been taken, the kidnappers will almost certainly be in touch."

Lipscombe left with a civil service handshake and Karl's contact details. Karl was not assured by the man's confidence and resented his self-assured demeanour in light of the lack of information about Peter.

Karl called Jean Claude after lunch, but there was little information he could tell the Al Jazeera editor apart from the destination hotel in Kandahar.

"He said he was going to the hills," said Jean Claude, "but the hills in Afghanistan - it is all hills. We talked about Helmand, and I know he was going to drive to Kandahar with Mika Hassan, the driver and translator we have used many times. He told the receptionist at his hotel on Friday that they were leaving."

"And if he *has* been taken, do we know where the kidnappers would have come from?" asked Karl.

"Probably they are from Afghanistan," said Jean Claude.

"I mean where they are they based. Where they are hiding."

"OK. It was likely that the abductors had approached from the opposite direction, and if Peter and Mika did not get all the way to Kandahar, they will be in the Zabul province, probably. This is not a known Taliban area, and is being handed over to Afghan security forces."

"Have you heard anything from your contacts?" Karl asked.

"No. I have a few contacts, but who they are is not something I can share with you. And no one has told me anything. OK, of course this may change."

"Thank you, Jean Claude," said Karl.

"Well, I hope for him."

"We all do."

Karl hung up the phone and looked at the handset, hoping it would ring. He knew Peter would have called if he had access to his phone. He made his last call in Kabul before the weekend and then the trail went cold, a wind covered the tracks with dust, and the valleys, with the bandits above them, held their silence.

#

Sarah smiled at Carla and pushed the button to the sixth floor. Sarah was running late and had not eaten the breakfast for which she had little appetite.

Her favourite part of the each day had become the moment just after she woke, before she remembered that Peter was missing - when she was unaware of the pit of her stomach, before the dawning of an unknown danger, before the world stood still briefly and then resumed without her.

Jim called out to her as she walked past News. "Sarah, do you have a second?"

"Can I take my jacket off first, please?" she said without stopping.

"Yes, of course, sorry."

Sarah felt sorry for her terse reply, and Jim regretted calling out to her before she had reached her desk, but he wanted to clear what little air there was between them.

She walked to her desk, took off her jacket and put her bag on the floor next to her chair. Jim stood up and spoke to Carla about the news running order. Sarah turned on her computer without sitting down and looked at him across the four rows of desks. He took the signal and walked towards her desk, wearing an expression of inquiry and pointing behind her to the meeting room at the end of the department.

"In here OK?" he said.

She nodded, turned and followed him in. She closed the door behind her.

"I wanted to say sorry," he said. Sarah didn't respond. "I didn't mean to imply you did anything wrong. I'm not even really involved in this."

"No," she said, "but I am. I sent the email."

"Yes you did," he said, glancing briefly at the ground so it didn't look like he was accusing her, "- and you are. Involved, I mean. You, the Foreign

Office, Karl, the Army, whoever else, I don't know. I'm no one in this and it's not my place to judge you."

"It's OK," she said with guarded warmth. "You're his friend and you're worried."

He felt grateful for her understanding. He thought Peter, wherever he was, was a lucky man to have her concern. He hoped he would treat her with respect, unlike Judith in Travel, who no one thought had a heart but wore it like an armband when she told Sarah about the "break up" - her actual words - of her and Peter.

"We're all worried," said Jim.

"Yes we are." Sarah forced a smile.

"Thank you. And again, I'm sorry."

She walked past him and sighed with relief and let out a cough that shuddered slightly in sadness. She touched his arm as he held the door open for her and she wondered if it was the role of those most afflicted to comfort the ones who suffer less.

Jim returned to his desk and Sarah logged into her PC.

Date: 22 August 2010. 14:32:08 GMT+1
From: UKPeterBeckenham@yahoo.co.uk
To: Sarah.Copland@corp.npl.com
Subject: Re: U OK?
Message:

Peter Beckenham and his driver Mika Hassan are being held by our organisation and we wish to come to the arrangement of $10 million US paid in cash to exchange for their safe and quick release. This amount is not for negotiation. When you confirm your cooperation we will discuss details.

Her heart pounded in her neck and her mouth dried. Her eyes flashed to the icon of a video attachment, which she clicked to open and the blood drained from her face as the image of Peter and another man appeared. She hit the pause button and the video froze a second after his voice came from her speakers.

Sarah didn't seem to stand up before breaking into a run, a thundering burst of bangles with each sudden movement while her colleagues looked for the source of the noise. Running inside was an unusual sound for a morning. Jim thought at first that the footfalls were a cascade of books sliding and falling off a desk, perhaps onto a bag, with the soft impact and flap of fabric. Then he saw her, sprinting through the Editorial department like she was being chased.

She was struggling to breathe as she ran past him. The chair in her wake was spinning from where it had hit the wall of the meeting room behind her desk. He knew it was Peter. He watched her open Karl's door. The Editorial Director stood up quickly. Her back was to the department floor and the staff near his office watched them. She slammed the door shut behind her and they saw her bring her hands to her face as Karl helped her to a chair.

24
Monday 23 August 2010
Zabul Province

A knock on the door roused Peter from a light sleep. Mika woke to the sound of the tray being placed on the table between the couches as Samir delivered an approximation of an English cooked breakfast, made up of slim, spicy sausage with fried eggs, warm flat bread and chickpeas. Samir nodded to them, almost graciously, as he put the food on the table.

"They will not kill us, I think," said Mika after Samir left. Peter admired his optimism. "No one has threatened us since the video."

"It's been two days. Do you think we have some bargaining power?" said Peter.

"I think so, yes. They have no advantage. And you see," Mika motioned towards the food, "they made us sausages. With eggs. They are not animals. I believe we are safe."

Peter dipped a sausage into a yolk. "That's good thinking," he said.

Mika smiled and Peter returned it.

"And you got all that from breakfast?" said Peter. "Maybe *you* should be the hack."

Mika laughed.

Peter continued, "That's it, *I'm* driving us home when we leave here. You've got five hundred words on sustainable energy. 'Green Power In A Brown Land'. You'll get three minutes on the Six." Peter chuckled to himself. "Singing in the lifeboats," he said quietly.

They grinned into their breakfasts.

Wahid and Zia entered a few minutes later. Wahid sat down in the armchair while Peter kept eating. Zia stood by the door as Wahid spoke. "Peter, there has been no news coverage of your disappearance."

"There won't be," said Peter, pushing some chickpeas onto his bread without looking up. "Because I'm not important."

"I do not believe you," said Wahid.

Peter finished a mouthful hurriedly. "I don't work for anyone."

"And the BBC? NPL? Al Jazeera?"

"None of them are taking my stories. Al Jazeera ran *one* video piece. That's it. It wasn't even a good story."

"You are a good journalist?" he asked. Mika started eating again, more for the appearance of composure than hunger.

"I'm all right," said Peter, "but it doesn't matter." He looked around the room. "This isn't a good story. This will be kept out of the media. I guarantee it. Running my story will only encourage other kidnappings."

"No one cares that you are missing," said Wahid. He wanted to challenge Peter, to taunt him like he did with the whore of NPL comment.

Peter put down his fork. "Exactly. And no one cares who we were captured by." He enjoyed saying it. *We can make another video if you want to,* he thought, *it doesn't matter - and fuck you.*

Wahid's posture stiffened and Zia moved forward, sensing the tone of Peter's comment and the offence it had caused, but Wahid brushed the air to motion him back. Zia dropped his shoulders and seethed in the doorway.

Peter continued. "You don't want to attract attention, but you're trying to get the money. You don't want war, but you're trying to build fear. This isn't an investment, Wahid - this is a gamble, and it's not a good one. If you kill me, I will become 'Peter Beckenham, the dead British journalist'. You are not terrorists yet, but if we are harmed you will become the enemy. You will be seen as Al Qaeda sympathisers. My steps will be traced and you will be hunted."

Mika swallowed and he watched his companion.

Peter leaned forward. "No one wants this story," he said. "If you set us free, this problem will disappear like it never existed. We are ghosts, Wahid. There will only be a story if I die, and if I do, your death will follow.

Wahid said something in a sharp growl, which Peter presumed was a curse. Mika looked at Zia, expecting the aggressor to react, which he did by inching forward with the slow, settled purpose of a ship starting to move.

Peter spoke again, more clearly, with calm enunciation.

"If you kill Mika, you'll start a diplomatic incident with Egypt. The Afghan government will look for justice - revenge maybe - I don't know."

"And what about you?" said Wahid. "What about Sarah?"

"Me? Her life will go on, but I can't say the same about you and your son. And until then, if that day ever comes, I'm just a guy in a room, and a story no one wants."

Wahid turned to Mika who shrugged in agreement and absolution. Wahid instructed Zia and they both stood up. Peter rose from his chair and Zia stepped forward and closer to Peter. He felt a fist pound him in the stomach and the room empty itself of air. Zia stood over Peter briefly as he writhed on the floor, and the two men left.

25
Tuesday 24 August 2010
Hammersmith

Adam Lipscombe went over the points he was going to make when he called Karl. The Foreign Office training course entitled "Hostage Protocol and Concerned Party Liaison" was still fresh in his mind from the seminar held a few months earlier and he had briefed his manager after his visit to NPL's offices the day before.

"Good morning Mr. Howard," he said, "this is Adam Lipscombe, Foreign and Commonwealth Office. How are you?"

"I'm all right," said Karl, moving the telephone closer to him while he held the receiver to his ear, "but increasingly worried about Peter, obviously. Can we say things are desperate now?"

"Well," said Lipscombe, "let's look at the situation. I've seen the video sent from Mr. Beckenham's Yahoo account. We have been working very closely with the company to keep abreast of developments and by monitoring incoming and outgoing emails, we can check login activity and the location data of whoever accesses the account."

"That's good news."

"It's a start. We know the account was accessed on a PC somewhere between Qalat and Kandahar, and Yahoo says the account is being checked twice a day from the same location."

"Does this help us devise a plan of action?" asked Karl. "If we know the area where he is being held and they are waiting to hear back, can't we act on that?"

"Unfortunately, there isn't that much that we didn't know before. This still doesn't allow us to pinpoint the kidnappers in what has been a largely peaceful region."

"But we do know he has been kidnapped and we have their demands."

"A ransom request was always the likely scenario," said Lipscombe.

"Despite you denying it yesterday," said Karl.

"I didn't deny it. I said we could only deal with the scenario in front of us."

"Well, how does this end, then," Karl said impatiently, "this scenario? Because you're going to tell me that giving in to their demands makes the hostage-taking economy look very lucrative."

"Mr. Howard, the video bears none of the hallmarks of known terrorist organisations. We've liaised with sources in the US State Department and Afghan security authorities."

"That doesn't mean he's not in danger."

"No, it doesn't, but in this scenario-"

"Look, I've had enough of scenarios. We're talking about a friend of mine. Just because this doesn't play out alongside one of your precedents doesn't mean we're in control of the situation. You're going to suggest we do nothing, aren't you?"

"Mr. Howard. We're reviewing the situation day by day. If we learn anything new I'll be in touch."

"You said that before, and then we learned this."

"And now we know even more," said Lipscombe. " I know this is frustrating for you, but just as you understand why covering this story could put Mr. Beckenham at risk, if we give in to their demands, it could encourage many more kidnappings of civilians in the region."

"Well I'm not giving in. I'm going to talk to the board about this situation and discuss the ransom money."

"At this stage, a financial settlement wouldn't be wise. I know it's difficult."

"Are we finished?" said Karl.

"Call me if you need anything. Please don't hesitate."

"Have you got ten million dollars?"

"Mr. Howard, I hope the Government's position on this matter is clear."

"Perfectly."

26
Tuesday 24 August 2010
Zabul Province

Mika was reading a five-week-old copy of
Newsweek from a newly deposited pile of magazines,
which Samir had placed on the shelf under the stand
of the disconnected television. The translator had
already read through the News section and was
reading the Sports pages; full of baseball players he
didn't know and batting averages he couldn't
understand. In Arts and Entertainment sections, the
writers of Saturday Night Live were going on strike,
he read, but he had never seen the show.

Peter finished flicking through a Time magazine,
which he hadn't absorbed. "So do we just wait? I'm
not that good at waiting," he said.

Mika turned a page.

"You're going to say 'Insha'Allah' or something
aren't you?" said Peter.

"I wasn't going to say it."

"See-" Peter shuffled in the armchair and folded
the magazine in half. "What gets me about that is that
people use god's will as a way of accepting their
failings and disappointment with life while they are
waiting around for success."

"Is this predicament our failing?" asked Mika.

"The whole faith thing," said Peter, "it's like an app
for your misfortune. 'Things are crappy. Will they
turn around? *If it's god's will*.'"

"Not always," said Mika.

"I *get* it. I mean, I get that circumstances beyond
our control throw us to the four winds and we just
have to suck it up, but anticipating it with a branded

hope is just stupid. 'We've had three straight days of rain. Will we get a fourth? *If it's god's will.*' That's easier to deal with, because it's down to things beyond our control and there's an element of chance. It's the universe playing dice with god. What I can't accept is that our situation was in any way either preordained or can be resolved by a higher force. And either way, Wahid's take on it is completely different. He's probably wondering if it's god's will for the ransom to be paid. It's all relative and subjective and human. The only hand any of us are touched by also touches money, war and technology. That doesn't sound like god to me."

Peter wasn't taking his own argument particularly seriously; he was talking more to pass the time, to keep his mind active in the monotony of what he saw as long and hopeless days.

"I do not think Wahid is thinking this," said Mika.

"Why not?"

"The Pashtun people," said Mika, "are fatalists, but they don't meet it with resignation."

"So events are determined but you're allowed to smile every now and then?"

"It's more that they believe that god knows what will happen, but a man alone can fix it."

Peter squinted his eyes and attempted a New York accent: "'*God's been a real sport to me.*'"

Mika frowned for an explanation.

"Dead Zone?" asked Peter.

Mika pouted and nodded once, but only up. It was half a nod, and backwards, inviting an explanation.

"The film? OK. Christopher Walken, right? He plays this character that can look into the future and see how people's lives will play out. But it's a double-edged thing, because even though it's great, it gives him a responsibility he'd rather not have. It's a mixed blessing. So when he tells someone about it, and this guy goes 'god has given you this gift' or something, he says sarcastically 'Oh yeah, god's been a real sport to me.'"

Mika drew his lips thinner in comprehension as he thought what to say next.

"It just reminded me of that," said Peter, "the whole thing about god serving up people's fortunes. Blessings... smitings.... it's just another day at the office for god."

"They have a saying in Pashto: 'Man alone can change his fate'."

"Then it's not destiny, is it? It's watered down - it's like homeopathic fatalism."

Mika closed his magazine. "There is a man from Afghanistan," he said, "who lives in Las Vegas. He moved there during the war with the Russians because it was not safe to stay. He is Pashtun and he works in the MGM hotel, in the casino on the machines. The machines?" Mika put his right arm in front of him and pulled it back.

"Slot machines?"

"Slot machines, yes. His name is Amanullah Naqshabandi."

"Did he win?" asked Peter. He hurried to answer his own question, "Hang on: he *won* but kept working there. Ooh - he won, but he gave it all *away*."

Mika shook his head. "No, he did not win. He is forbidden as a Muslim to gamble."

"Right, OK. And how does he feel helping people gamble?"

"He says he leaves it to god."

Peter screwed up one side of his mouth in a half conviction. "I don't buy it. He knows the rules. He's read the back of the box, but he's using an unknown entity to absolve himself of responsibility."

"For him it's not unknown. He stands before Allah."

"That's bullshit. It's like killers on the stand who tell the courtroom that only god can judge them. 'Actually, no, the law and the people will judge you. God does whatever you think.'"

"But you take an oath on the bible, no?"

"You do, although actually you can choose not to, but you shouldn't go against your principles and profess your innocence," said Peter.

"He's not saying he is innocent," said Mika. He is saying he is willing to be accountable."

Peter sat up growing, more agitated. "You can't do whatever the fuck you want and wait for a cosmic audit one day," he said. "Even if this guy did, and god forgave him, he would have enabled thousands of people to gamble, and that's something he knows is wrong. Unless he doesn't think it's wrong and therefore has no faith in his own beliefs."

"It is a moral dilemma."

"Well, it sounds to me like he made a convenient compromise."

"Perhaps," said Mika.

"Don't get me wrong," said Peter. "I don't care about gambling. I think adults can do what they like. It's a thin line between investment and gambling. I don't like it being called 'gaming' but that's another story. But the responsibility lies with the individual."

Peter unfolded the copy of Time, scanned the cover and considered opening the magazine again. He looked back at Mika. "I thought we were talking about fate."

"I was coming to that," said Mika.

The answer made Peter laugh. "Does this man think he was predestined to work the slots at the MGM?" he asked.

"He does."

"Unbelievable. There was a war, he emigrated to a country that granted him entry, and he found a job opening. It's a complete game of chance. A crapshoot. He out of anyone should know that."

"Maybe he does."

"Why would he try to improve his situation at all if it's simply god's plan?" asked Peter.

"I remember the words he used. He said: 'I am here because of his destiny and all I can do is make the best of my situation.' Do you understand?"

Peter inspected the bars on the windows and gazed at the sky on the other side. "I'm starting to."

27
Wednesday 25 August 2010
Zabul Province

"Do you speak English, Samir?"

The gunman had brought scrambled eggs.

"It's Samir, right?" said Peter. "Eggs for breakfast, thank you," he continued as Samir set down the tray. "Tea, bread - look at that, Mika."

Samir looked at Mika. "This is Mika," said Peter. "Samir? Do you speak English?"

"A little," he said softly.

"That's very good," said Peter quietly.

Mika took a plate.

"Are you the man who is going to kill me, Samir?" said Peter.

Samir understood and looked hurt and horrified, as if in a sudden concern.

Mika glanced at Peter, who shot him a hopeful smile that was only with the eyes.

"Samir, this isn't our destiny," said Peter. Samir shook his head furtively. "Does Wahid understand this?"

Samir moved the tea and the remaining plate from the tray to the space on the table while he thought. "You are not the enemy," he said. He looked at the doorway, turned back to Peter, and added, "You must not escape."

Mika whispered to him, little more than mouthing the word. "Zia?"

Samir nodded to both of them, almost bowed, and walked out, closing the door behind him.

Peter and Mika hadn't planned to escape, although they had discussed the idea of it. They doubted they would be shot, because they knew they would be worthless dead, but even if they were successful, an Egyptian and a British man in southern Afghanistan would be too conspicuous on foot, and Peter couldn't tell where the loyalties of the Zabul locals rested. He didn't know if he and his guide would even make it to the road, or where the road was, apart from downhill and into the valley and the unknown.

He was certain, however, that NPL would not pay any ransom, whatever the amount. He had let his hope slip away gently over the days, and he only noticed it had faded completely when it was gone.

He felt let down and cheated. NPL had supported him like a family through personal crises. It had sent him a case of wine when he won the award for Online News Editor Of The Year in 1998.

It was Karl who told Peter his mother had been hit by a bus. He made the call on a summer evening in 1997, the day after Peter's last conversation with her. "If anything happens to me, you know I love you," she said, before dying on the street, in the rain, with him the only person she knew in England, and less than a mile from where she fell. He was twenty-four at the time and she was two months short of her fiftieth birthday.

Peter had just arrived home from work when the phone rang.

"The police have said she was in an accident on the Great West Road," Karl explained. "They have your number and they are going to contact you. Do you understand?"

"You're saying I should just wait."

"That's right. Do you want me to come over? I can be there in twenty minutes."

"Do you know anything? Do I have to go somewhere?"

"Just sit tight. The police will be in touch."

Peter thought about his next question, and how best to frame it. "In person?"

"I don't know, mate." Karl didn't tell Peter what condition his mother was in, but he knew Peter would assume he was checking to see if he was home so the police could make a house call, and that house calls were made for critical cases and deaths.

One of the witnesses at the inquest said she was pushed into the road. Another said she was running in the middle of the bus lane. Someone on the other side of the street said she moved to the front of the pack of people waiting to cross the street and she adjusted her handbag before putting her hands by her side and falling forward calmly, face down like a weary traveller into a soft hotel bed, under the wheels of a double decker bus.

A weary traveller. He thought it was a fitting analogy. The previous day she had taken the train from her home in Wales and checked into a hotel in London and tried to convince that him that someone was trying to kill her. He dismissed it as paranoia, said he loved her and left her room. She looked afraid and it scared him. Their last conversation had ended strangely, but it came into sharp focus when Karl called his flat to tell him about the accident.

After a few minutes a police car pulled up outside Peter's flat. He was already putting his shoes on as the officers climbed the stairs to his front door. He knew. He opened the door, invited them in before turning down the hall, walking away from them, back into the living room to sit down.

The two policemen stood in front of the couch, shoulder to shoulder like costumed singing telegrams. The younger officer looked barely twenty. *You poor fucker*, thought Peter. He guessed he couldn't have been more than a few months into the job. *It's OK.* The new constable was late in taking off his hat and when he did he looked like he was going to be sick into it. *I'm sorry.* The young man could barely look up.

Peter's next memory was of heading across London a few minutes later to make a formal identification. Sitting in the speeding car, he caught reflections of himself in shop widows, in strobes of red and blue lights, wondering with stillness under the wailing sirens how quickly they would make it across town in the rush hour traffic. Forty minutes? Twenty? Fifteen?

On the way through town someone announced on the police radio that "the victim" had been moved straight to the mortuary, and the driver responded, saying they were changing destination from the hospital and would head straight to the police station instead.

Peter walked up the back steps into the station where solemn silences suggested he had been expected and that the officers on duty knew why he was being ushered respectfully into an interview room.

Peter believed there are around ten moments, certainly no fewer than a dozen significant events in every person's life that shaped them as individuals, challenged their identities and the relationship they had with the world.

To him, the events didn't necessarily have to be disasters, although they would be among them. They could also be a birth of a child, or the fulfilment of a life goal, the chance answering of an epiphany, which had been ringing unanswered. He considered them to be like a door beyond which the rest of their life was waiting for them to walk through. He believed that it was all relative, and on a sliding scale of a bigger journey, but in every lifetime there were about ten defining moments.

The company had sheltered him when she died. Karl created a channel for the flow of information after the accident and organised a condolence card on his return to work. The senior editorial staff and those closest to him across the department, including Sarah and Jim, signed it. It was a dignified act of compassion and duty for a moment that happened when Peter was under NPL's wing.

He remembered vivid details of that rainy night - small brushstrokes that made a greater impact than the larger canvas. A bloodied passport. The smell of almond biscuits and her perfume on an oil-streaked purse. A handwritten letter saying she was finally ready to meet god and would no longer be afraid. The policeman handed Peter the two rings she had worn on the day she married his father. They were twisted and crushed flat like discarded ring pulls on a beach, and a single diamond clung to the smaller one like a barnacle.

Her fingers, he thought, the hands that once held me.

The police gave him back everything apart from his mother.

He went from the police station to her hotel and the manager gave him the key to her room. She had packed her bags and lifted them onto the bed, even though she had arranged to stay in London for a week. He carried her luggage down to the reception desk where the manager asked him apologetically if he would be paying the bill and on the additional charges he noticed a double vodka had been taken from the mini-bar at 10:40 that morning. She rarely drank anything stronger than wine but when she did it was a vodka and tonic, although never before dinner.

Back at his flat later that evening he started phoning the relatives. All of his immediate family lived out of the country, so he was the point of contact for the police and the personal taxi service for the relatives as they flew into Heathrow.

They put flowers on the railings at the scene of the accident on Brompton Road and on his bouquet of pink roses he wrote a note with a line from a Dolly Parton song, mostly because words had failed him. She didn't particularly like Dolly Parton, but he thought she was in keeping with the lyrics, an eagle when she flew, although she rarely did towards the end of her life.

At the coroner's inquest he met some of the witnesses who came forward, apart from the shop attendant who sat with her as she died. He wanted to thank her most of all, but she was off work for several weeks with the post-traumatic stress that must come from hanging on to a person who can't. He never knew what gave that young woman the courage to leave her shop and walk out into the wet evening to watch over a woman dying in the street and he hoped he never would, but she remained an anonymous inspiration in the years which followed. He never contacted her, but she gave him hope that he might one day be as brave.

He didn't know if he should have taken his mother to a psychiatric hospital when he had the chance. Peter felt she had become a danger to herself and he had called a doctor on the morning of the day she died, after visiting her hotel room and seeing how frightened and confused she was.

The doctor told him that no one would be able to help her unless he took her there by force, and Peter decided against that course of action and went to work as if it were any other day.

He sometimes looked back on it and wondered if he should have left her that night in her room, but he couldn't afford to have regrets. He believed that we act on what we know and we make our decisions based on the information we have at the time. *It's all we ever have*, he thought.

Four days after her death, he rented a van and drove over the Severn Bridge and on to her home to clear out her belongings. He unlocked the front door and walked in to smells of her and memories of his childhood. The house was just as she had left it, tidy and clean, with a note for him on her bed.

Before she died he used to think that tragedy somehow made people wiser, that it unlocked secret knowledge held by those who had truly lived, honing their faculties to better equip them for life. His mother had known tragedy in her time and it had done nothing to help her, and having seen it himself, Peter knew little more than to never give up. *Ever.* No matter what was going on around you, on winter nights you can't stand, through summer days you wish were shorter. *Never give up.*

28
Wednesday 25 August 2010
Hammersmith

Karl had been fielding calls all day, and the agenda to his media colleagues remained clear: this would not be reported. Adam Lipscombe had stressed that the Foreign Office didn't want a Ken Bigley situation, another hostage taken captive, paraded by the media and killed by his kidnappers when their demands weren't met.

The Foreign Office's apparent lack of compassion prompted Karl to call Mika Hassan's father. Peter had no living parents and no brothers or sisters and Karl wanted to show his support to at least one of the families. He arranged a time with the Egyptian Ministry for Health and Population to talk to Emad Hassan,

"Dr. Hassan, can I start by saying that my thoughts are with you throughout this ordeal. We're all finding it difficult."

"Thank you. I appreciate your sentiments, Mr. Howard. Tell me, please - do we know where my son is?"

Karl tried to sound reassuring, without venturing into optimism. "We know he's somewhere about an hour's drive north east of Kandahar. We don't think he is more than forty miles either side of the road to Kabul, possibly near the border of the Zabul and Kandahar provinces."

"So the military can start a search and rescue mission?"

"It's more complicated than it seems." Karl hated lying, but it was kinder than the wait-and-see tactics of the Foreign Office. "For a start, that's a big area. Secondly, this is not a military operation, as there's no clear evidence the kidnappers are members of any terrorist group."

"I'm aware of this from my discussion with William Hague."

Karl was surprised to learn that the British Foreign Secretary had taken the matter up personally. He thought Peter would be amused to know that cabinet members and almost certainly the Prime Minister had been discussing his disappearance. He wondered if William Hague would remember Peter from the live chat event he did with NPL at the fundraiser years before.

"This does not help me find my son, or return your friend," said Dr. Hassan.

"Not immediately," said Karl. "It's a long game." He hoped that the word *game* would not be taken literally - he dismissed the concern, seeing as the minister spoke English so fluently.

"How can *you* help?" asked Dr. Hassan.

"That's partly why I was calling. If there's anything on our side, we-"

"You are a journalist, am I correct?"

"I'm an editor. I run NPL's Editorial department in the UK."

"You can address millions of people with your service."

"Dr. Hassan, I'm sure the Foreign Secretary has explained to you the risks associated with publicising the situation."

"Mr. Howard, this is not something I can do. I can not pay ten million dollars and even if I were to make this a political issue, it would not be reported due to your organisation's stranglehold on the news agenda."

"With respect, it's not a stranglehold. It's a conscious decision not to play into the hands of terrorists and a concerted effort by my colleagues in the media. Also, it's not entirely my idea."

"Then do it differently."

"But it's one I support," said Karl.

"You are hiding behind your government," said the minister.

"Believe me, sir, that's the last thing I would do."

"This man, your-"

"-Peter Beckenham."

"He is not your son."

"No, but I assure you the decision wouldn't be any more difficult if he were my own brother. We can not risk their lives."

"He is already in danger!" Dr. Hassan said loudly.

"We need more information."

"Mr. Howard - I have a story as well."

Karl waited.

"My story is about NPL being reluctant to act over one of their unnamed journalists being held hostage."

"That's not the truth," said Karl.

"Does that always stop you, Mr. Howard?"

"Personally, yes."

"Well, it might be different when they steal your son. My own story is about NPL covering up a kidnapping, and the British government telling the military not to intervene. The tabloid press would like this very much."

"Dr. Hassan, from everything we know, exposure would put your son and my friend at risk."

"We will see."

"Sir, I would ask you not to take -"
"Good morning, Mr. Howard."
The line went dead.

29
Wednesday 25 August 2010
Zabul Province

Peter knew that Karl would keep Jean-Claude informed about his situation and both men would respect the media sensitivity alert. Even if Al Jazeera could contact Wahid, Peter was confident that it wouldn't, because it would put a premium on his value as a captive. These thoughts didn't bring him closer to freedom, but it was a small comfort to understand the flow of information behind the scenes.

There was shouting upstairs that evening, around midnight. Male voices were raised, muffled behind walls and amplified by the darkness. Peter and Mika stood huddled by the door. Wahid and Zia's voices, he was sure. Then a woman's voice, followed by Wahid. The woman answered. There was a shout before a child's calling. It was a young voice, perhaps five or six, clearer in tone, sounding coherent and insecure. The woman rebuked the men then explained something to the child in a consoling tone.

"What are they saying?" Peter whispered.

Mika was listening intently, giving a hushed commentary as he crouched next to the wooden door. Peter stood in the dark behind him.

A man shouted, and Mika translated softly in a hushed commentary: "'...this was not your idea! The plan is mine...'"

"Wahid?" asked Peter quietly.

Mika swatted the question away, and translated a bark. "'...No one will know.' 'You can't be sure.' 'No one knows already...'"

"Knows what? If we live or die?"

"Shhh." A child shouting. "'...Please. When?...'" The female voice. *"'...And how long?' 'Answers'...* Something about answers, about waiting for a reply..."

The shouting died down, dipping in a sadness that suggested to Peter a resignation, a conceded solidarity. The voices faded to tones without syllables and Mika lost the meaning as the quiet returned, broken by footsteps on the stairs past the kitchen behind the door.

Peter and Mika hurried back to their sofas and threw the blankets over themselves like naughty children at a sleepover. They expected a knock at the door and they pretended they were asleep.

Several minutes passed and the sound of sporadic footsteps died down. A goat in the valley pronounced an accusatory bleat while Peter and Mika discussed the commotion.

"...A response to the email Wahid would have sent," Peter ventured quietly.

"Or a media response to our kidnapping," said Mika. "They said 'No one knows'."

"Who said?"

"The woman. No one knows *about us being here*?"

"Is that a good thing?" asked Peter.

"I don't know. We're alive. That's good."

"I'm not sure anyone knows about us being *here*, but they know we aren't where we would otherwise be, which is in Kandahar, said Peter. "They know we're missing, and they aren't reporting it or they aren't replying."

30
Wednesday 25 August 2010
Hammersmith

By late afternoon, Karl was on his fifth coffee of the day and resolving it would be his last. He would not have told Adam Lipscombe about his conversation with Dr. Hassan had he not been desperate. He knew that part of the responsibility of editorial power was being able to tell when he was out of his depth. He didn't want to have a diplomatic argument with a member of a foreign government, but he wasn't above letting others do it.

Knowing that going to the press with the story of *not* publishing Peter's situation was as dangerous as running the story itself, he relayed Dr. Hassan's intentions to Lipscombe.

Sarah burned with the urge to answer the kidnappers' email, but Karl had explained that the abduction was in danger of becoming an international diplomatic concern. Peter Beckenham and Mika Hassan were becoming an even bigger story, headliners out of the headlines.

The identity of the kidnappers remained a mystery, even to those closest to the story. Jean Claude had been able to determine through informed Al Jazeera sources that Al Qaeda wasn't holding them. He told Karl, who was reassured by this more than he was by the noises coming from the US State Department via the Foreign office. He suspected the Americans were happy for Peter to remain in captivity so they could study how the events unfolded and record another scenario for future abduction situations.

"Do you believe that Dr. Hassan would go to the newspapers with the details of the abduction?" asked Lipscombe during his regular phone briefing with Karl at the end of the day.

"I'm not certain," said Karl. "There's a risk. And media blackout or not, his angle is the kind of media conspiracy that bloggers love. They could angle it so it looked like NPL fired Peter and hung him out to dry in Afghanistan. Dr. Hassan is frustrated, like the rest of us. If he picked the right paper and left out enough specific details, I think someone would run it."

"It's possible," said Lipscombe.

Karl continued, "This sounds like a government issue. I don't want to get involved - I'm just bringing it up as a concern."

"Thank you, Mr. Howard. It sounds like a matter for the Foreign Secretary's further attention."

"Can he tell an Egyptian cabinet minister what he can and can't do?"

"Not in so many words, but there is pressure we can apply."

Karl wondered what this meant, but knew Lipscombe wouldn't tell him if he asked.

"I do have *some* good news about Peter," said Karl.

"Excellent. What's that?"

"I have it on the best authority that Peter's kidnappers are not members of the Taliban or Al Qaeda."

The line went quiet for a moment. "How do you know that?" asked Lipscombe.

"I sent the clip to the Editor of Al Jazeera English in Dubai, a man I trust implicitly. He confirmed what I think the US State Department and MI5 already suspected - these men have no apparent ties to any known enemy or terrorist organisation," said Karl.

"You sound fairly sure."

"If they were part of a bigger group he would know, believe me," said Karl.

"What's this man's name, out of interest?"

"Jean Claude Charbonneau. He used to work here as my predecessor. He has a great number of reliable contacts, not all of them savoury characters, and sources he'll of course want to keep confidential."

"Well, that is reassuring news."

"But we have to wait some more?" said Karl.

"I'm afraid we must."

"Great," said Karl sarcastically, although without cruelty.

"Mr. Howard, you are doing everything you can. I appreciate that - keeping this out of the media is no small job, but it goes a long way towards ensuring Mr. Beckenham and Mr. Hassan's safe return," said Lipscombe.

"That much I *can* do. I don't wield an influence over the Egyptian cabinet ministers, though."

"You can leave that one with us."

Karl asked the question anyway. "What exactly can you do? Do I want to know?"

Lipscombe laughed. "It's nothing clandestine, I can tell you that. Just good old-fashioned diplomacy."

"And you'll do this personally?" Karl was beginning to warm to Lipscombe, and didn't want him to feel that he thought he was incapable. The Editorial Director was genuinely intrigued by the inner workings of international relations.

"Oh no, not at all," said Lipscombe, "this one is best handled by an organisation with a bit of clout.

Someone who could have a friendly word in Dr. Hassan's ear and convince him that's he's picking the wrong battles. In the nicest possibly way, of course. The Foreign and Commonwealth Office only handles international diplomacy, not matters of personal interest, but Dr. Hassan could be advised by a third party that his talents lie in politics and not in feeding his opinions to the media. Someone, and I couldn't possibly say who, will remind him that his efforts should be concentrated elsewhere.

"Not our guys, though?"

"I believe they call it 'blowing smoke up his ass'," he said.

"The Americans?"

"...it's a vulgar term. MI5 wouldn't approve."

"The fucking *CIA*?" Karl laughed. He rarely swore outside of close relationships but the scale of the situation amused him. In the past week, his friend had gone missing, the Prime Minister had been briefed, Karl had an argument with a member of the Egyptian cabinet and the CIA was stepping in to smooth things over.

"Mr. Howard, I must go. If I hear anything at all, I'll keep you informed."

"Thank you, Adam," he said, using his name for the first time.

"I hope I've been of some help."

"It's been," Karl hesitated in his amusement, "it's been very enlightening."

31
Thursday 26 August 2010
Zabul Province

Mika read the previous week's Herald Tribune while Peter ate his bread and finished his coffee. Out of context, the setting appeared to him almost serene. He thought things could be worse, that people elsewhere in the world were being held in dreadful conditions. There were innocent people being killed in gang vengeance, people traded in slavery, or families born into debt. On the scale of global human adversity, he reasoned, his situation was nowhere near as bad.

In any crisis, he never considered the unknown as an enemy and would always look to his present situation, however awful, and measure it against something worse before gathering strength from his advantage. It wasn't a conscious strategy as much as a predisposed outlook, and in his current circumstances as long as he was fed, warm and valued alive, he felt well enough not to resent the time's passing.

"Question for you," he said.

Mika looked up from the newspaper. "Yes."

"Why did you become a translator?" Peter squinted at him quizzically.

Mika let the newspaper fall to his knees and went into a sudden contemplation, cocking his head to an angle like a dog hearing a distant noise for the first time.

"I don't know why I am a translator. My written language skills are not excellent. I enjoy travelling and would not like to work in an office. I like people and I have no family of my own. Like many journalists, I believe."

"I'm not a huge fan of people myself," said Peter, "at least not compared to many journalists. But as a breed we tend to be solitary, although I'm probably too much that way."

"Not so much that you are unwilling to share it."

"Fair point," said Peter.

"I would enjoy being a journalist one day perhaps."

"You need the written skills if you're going to be a reporter. Otherwise there is the production side, but then you've got to hate everybody."

"Really?" said Mika.

"No," said Peter. "That was a joke."

"I understand."

"A sense of humour's important, too."

Mika thumbed the edges of the newspaper.

"But why not, you know?" said Peter. "You have experience. You're old getting into it, but you've seen a lot of events. And *this*, being kidnapped? It's kind of a big deal."

"So you have found your story after all," said Mika.

"It is strange not to be the observer for a change. I keep seeing this situation as something that would happen to someone else, like a story I would report on instead of happening to me. It's odd. Maybe it's habit. Maybe it's a defence mechanism."

Peter felt more comfortable writing about events that happened to other people than living them himself.

"The morning of the London tube bombings," he said, "you know - 7/7? 2005?"

Mika nodded.

"Well I was at my desk when it happened. Hammersmith, in west London."

"Yes."

"So the story broke and we ran a splash and I-"

"A splash?"

"A news flash, an online announcement. It's like a headline graphic at the top of the screen."

"OK."

"Anyway, I was waiting for pictures and a story to come in."

Peter had known the terrorists would attack London eventually. The trains that week had been crawling with police sniffer dogs, but alerts often came and went and he thought little of it as he made his way to work. As usual, on the morning of 7 July 2005 he was at his desk deciding which stories to run with.

Sometimes he imagined he was reporting on events that weren't real. It was a coping tactic on the days when he slipped into thinking he made a life largely from the misery of others.

Not all stories were tragedies, he knew that, but when a disaster struck he watched the casualty figures roll before they were published and he looked at them like sport scores or share prices. They were important, but he didn't allow it to mean a great deal to him personally or how else he was supposed to think.

To him it was "text, pictures, and publish". Load, safety off, and fire.

On the morning of 7/7, his defence mechanism was breached. He updated the story after the bombs went off while the ambulances rushed by his window to rescue the dying and injured. He drew on toughness, but he wanted to hug someone.

Amid the sirens, on his screen, there were few pictures being filed from the scene fast enough to illustrate the events being reported. There were pictures filed within the hour, but they were all taken above ground from the point of view of the emergency services and the bystanders, and there was little from the perspective of the victims of the attacks below ground.

"The next morning, there were one or two shaky mobile phone videos," he told Mika, "but that was it. That was just five years ago. If that happened now, everyone would film everything about it. Every person there would have something on his or her Facebook page that morning. We may find that unusual now, but for the kid with the fake rocket launcher out there - Ali?"

"Ali, yes," said Mika.

"-right - that's all he *knows*. How old are you Mika?"

"Twenty nine."

"Twenty nine, OK, so just about. So, when we were kids, people didn't have the internet in their homes, obviously."

"Yes."

"We also both knew people who at some point in *their* youth didn't have a TV in their house, or electricity. Right? But *Ali*? He's used to technology, even out here, and American kids his age might grow up and tell kids he knew people who didn't have the *internet* when they were young."

"Or computers."

"Or even computers. Now there's this: when *we* were kids, we could watch newsreel footage, going back pretty much as far as you want - the Depression, the First World War, and there was a chance that the young people in those films were still alive."

"When we were children?"

"In the late 1970's, early 80's, yeah. The young men and women in that footage could have been alive when we were kids. Old men and women, maybe, but the point is that all of that film was shot within living memory."

"Quite possibly."

"Now imagine Ali looking at that. He wouldn't even imagine that someone in an old silent movie would be alive today."

"Of course."

"But isn't that strange?" asked Peter.

"Perhaps."

"Definitely. He can watch a film today and be

certain that everyone in the picture, from the wealthy gent to the grubby-faced, wide-eyed street urchin - is dead."

"Does it matter?"

"I think it does. He has absolutely no connection to a world before broadcasting. It's almost inconceivable to him that we, as kids, with the right leads, could have knocked on someone's door and asked what it was like to leave the deck of the Titanic the night it sank."

"Why does he need that connection?"

"Because it's personal. It's knowledge, not just information. It's slow-gained wisdom. Information travels fast now. He doesn't even have to look for it. Something happens and he just finds out. There's no discovery, no voyage, no personal exchange. It's just a flow of data."

"It's like a river."

"How do you mean?" said Peter.

"No past, just always on, always there, always flowing."

"When something is *happening* it's fast."

"Isn't something always happening?" asked Mika.

"Yes, but it's not always news."

"Like us."

"Yes," said Peter, "like us."

32
Thursday 26 August 2010
Hammersmith

"Is this Mr. Karl Howard of NPL?"

"Speaking." Karl looked away from his monitor and out the window. The telephone cord brushed over the invoices sitting on his desk.

"Mr. Howard," said the voice of a woman with a light Middle Eastern accent, "I am calling from the Egyptian Ministry for Health and Population. I have Cabinet Minister Dr. Emad Hassan on the line for you. I believe you spoke yesterday."

"We did, thank you."

"Is this a good time for you to talk?"

"Yes. It's fine, thank you."

There was a click and the ambient noise on the line changed timbre.

"Mr. Howard."

Karl recognised the long, slow, studied vowels bookended by clipped Arabic consonants.

"Dr. Hassan, good morning."

"I'm calling regarding our previous conversation."

The reference seemed unnecessary to Karl, having had only one prior interaction with the man, but the minister's formality rested on protocol. "Yes," was all he said.

"It appears I might have left you with the impression that I was going to take matters into my own hands."

"Dr. Hassan, I completely understand your frustration. It's a natural response for a father."

"I regret implying that it wasn't being handled well, and on reflection I am assured that the authorities are doing everything they can."

"Assured?" asked Karl. He wondered if he meant "satisfied", or "convinced".

"I understand that this is a security issue and a delicate matter," said Dr. Hassan. "I'd like you to know I would never do anything to put my son's life at risk."

"Of course."

"Excellent. I wanted to make that clear. Please, if you hear anything, you will let me know? Communication between Egypt and her allies is always open and that in itself is a comfort to me."

"I will, and we're all working towards Mika and Peter's safe release."

"Then I'll wish you good day, Mr. Howard."

"Thank you for calling, Dr. Hassan."

Karl tried to picture how the CIA could have intervened; if it had called President Mubarak and told him to keep his staff in line or talked to Dr. Hassan and told him his political ambitions would be supported when he challenged the increasingly unpopular head of state in a leadership contest.

Karl wondered if the minister had been presented with scenarios of hostage situations where media intervention had led to a brutal and tragic conclusion. He had no idea, and was content not to.

33
Thursday 26 August 2010
Dubai

Agent Randal Cohen hadn't acclimatised to the desert heat. His four years covering the Middle East as a CIA operative had been spent largely indoors in briefing rooms, compiling situation reports for its Langley headquarters while his field agents and local contacts gathered intelligence on the ground.

As a civilian agency, the CIA had no law enforcement powers. Any arrests needed to be made by local officials. The Agency was allowed to accompany the Dubai police, and Cohen was pleased to be involved in some practical fieldwork, despite wearing a dark suit in the forty-three degree sun. The heat sucked every comfort from the cool fibres of his jacket as he stepped from the silver Mercedes and walked to the doorway of the Al Jazeera office.

His partner Steven Jaworski climbed out of the second car and spoke to two younger men dressed in cargo pants and short-sleeved shirts.

The receptionist had received a call a few minutes earlier instructing her that she should direct Agents Cohen and Jaworski to Jean Claude Charbonneau, who had information about an ongoing security operation that urgently required the news organisation's full co-operation. When she said no one could see Jean Claude without an appointment, she was told that it related to a missing person in danger. The voice assured her that Mr. Charbonneau would be able to help them and that she was already costing them precious time.

The CIA believed that Jean Claude's assurance that the kidnappers were not terrorists suggested a deeper understanding of the situation than they would reasonably expect from an innocent third party. Adam Lipscombe and his counterparts in the United States could not explain how Jean Claude's information matched their own, nor could they determine how he could be so certain that neither Al Qaeda nor the Taliban were holding Peter.

This didn't matter to Agent Jaworski as he watched the editor being handcuffed in the middle of the newsroom. The police led him away by the arm, and Jaworski answered Jean Claude's only question with a Boston accent as broad as his chest, saying he was being arrested "for the endangerment of the lives of US nationals and those of its allies."

Jean Claude was marched past his office, where he told Natasha to call his wife Celine. She stammered her quiet consent and Jean Claude was taken to the cars outside and driven away.

Jean Claude Charbonneau was the only person at Al Jazeera who knew that Peter was missing, and the journalists in the newsroom had no doubt their editor was the upstanding model of a law-abiding man whose arrest could not have related to any criminal activity he would have committed consciously.

They discussed it in the kitchen that afternoon.

"Maybe there was a murder. Someone important to America and he is refusing to help them in order to protect his sources."

"A murder would have been reported on the wires," someone answered.

"A kidnapping," said another.

"People go missing all the time. Why would Jean Claude know anything about it?"

"He would if it were a journalist."

"Not really."

"If it were a journalist who was important enough to attract America's attention. Important enough to arrest him in front of all of us."

34
Friday 27 August 2010
Northern Pakistan

The Commander was checking his emails when his deputy knocked on the door.

"Sir, I have some information which I think will be of interest."

He turned away from the screen and looked towards the man who interrupted him. He preferred to receive important information in person, and he was eager to hear why his second in command needed his attention so urgently.

The mechanics of the organisation bore little resemblance to the one he had helped to create more than twenty years earlier, after the war with the Russians. Information moved faster, but since the attacks of September 11th his movements had been restricted. Communication remained efficient but recruitment was difficult due to the greater need for security, despite the increased profile of the group.

The Al Qaeda network of terror cells which started in the Middle East and had stretched into Asia and Europe like an organism, like ivy on a wall, the roots obscured and almost incidental as each strand became more resourceful and self sustaining.

"What is the information?" He adjusted his robe as he moved his chair away from the desk.

"On Tuesday we were contacted by our communications operative who is an associate of the editor of Al Jazeera's English service in Dubai. The editor was asking about a British journalist who had gone missing on his route from Kabul to Kandahar."

"We have no current hostage operations in Zabul or Kandahar."

"That's correct, sir."

"So why does this journalist concern me?" The Commander looked impatient.

"There are two reasons. The first is that a man named Mika Hassan, whose father is the Egyptian Minster for Health and Population, accompanies him. The second is that one of their journalists told the operative that the Editor was arrested yesterday over his suspected involvement and the process was supervised by the CIA."

"Is there any chance this man is involved in the kidnapping?"

"Our operative says there isn't."

The Commander snorted. "The fools. They are unable to capture our blessed soldiers, so they arrest editors simply for talking to us."

"Sir, if the CIA is arresting people for asking questions about the disappearance of a British man, it suggests that this journalist is an important person, and whoever is holding him would stand to benefit from a large reward."

"I am aware of that. Why have we not heard of this in news programmes?"

"Our contact says there have been restrictions on reporting it," said the deputy

"This is no ordinary man. The media is keeping silent about their colleague and the Americans are arresting people who make inquiries about it. What is his name, this journalist?"

"Peter Beckenham."

"He should not be held by any group that is outside of our family."

"Precisely," said the deputy, hoping his affirmation would not be taken as insolence. To restore the balance, he added, "What do you recommend we do?"

The Commander sat up tall and touched his beard in thought. "There will be justice. Such operations must take place only with the consent of our organisation. We have built a strong army against the Crusaders and we must not be challenged. Our network operates together or not at all."

He stood up. The deputy bowed once and listened to his orders.

"The punishment of these so called Jihadist is the right action to strengthen our influence in the southern territories and send a message across our network and to its opponents. Find them - and make an example of them. Show these farm-dwelling Afghanis that they should stick to herding goats."

35
Friday 27 August 2010
Zabul Province

Peter and Mika tried not to discuss their situation beyond the nearest point of drudgery, but it seemed inevitable once the video had been shot, the demands had been made and there was nothing to do but wait.

"You know why the media will keep our disappearance out of the news," said Peter.

"Because we aren't important?" asked Mika.

"It's because reporting the story will *give* us an importance which will make Wahid think we are worth more money - that is, if he has actually asked for money."

"I think he has on his email."

"He probably has."

Peter felt sick at the thought that the video would probably have been sent to Sarah. If the media blackout had been effective enough to deter people from emailing him, he knew Wahid would pick an NPL employee from the few with whom he had kept in touch in recent weeks, and Sarah would be at the top of that short list of people most likely to reply.

He agreed with the need for reporting restrictions, and he hoped Twitter didn't light up with #FreeNPLPeter as a trending topic from concerned users sending support messages.

Mika stood on his toes for a glimpse out of the window and into the valley below.

"It's funny, though, isn't it," said Peter, "how in the middle of this age of communication, our situation is being discussed but not broadcast."

"Are you sure it's even being discussed?"

"Of course," said Peter. He adopted an Austrian accent. "Who is your daddy - and what does he do?"

Mika stared at Peter's expectant smile and said, "I'm sorry, I don't understand."

Peter lowered his pitch half an octave and laid the accent on with a trowel. "*Who iz y'deddy - and wut duz he doo?*"

Mika stared back at Peter.

"Kindergarten *Cop*?" asked Peter.

Mika shook his head.

"Oh come *on*," he pleaded. "Arnold Schwarzenegger? Where are your cultural references? OK, your father's an Egyptian cabinet minister and I'm a journalist. I left my job and people will be asking about me if they don't know I'm out here. 'Where did Peter end up?' 'He went to Afghanistan.' 'Really, who's he working for?' 'No one - that's just it. And no one has heard from him.'"

"'And he is with Sarah now, I hear'," said Mika.

"Yes, very good," said Peter. It was the first time he had heard his companion tell a joke. "People *are* talking about you and me."

"I hope it helps," said Mika.

"We just need the involvement of the right people. And for the wrong ones to stay out of the picture."

"Who are the wrong ones?" asked Mika.

"Wahid and these guys are not terrorists. At least we have that on our side. Actual terrorists would be the wrong ones."

There had been more furtive discussions that afternoon outside the door, muffled in heated tones that grew clearer and stopped when Zia delivered their food. There was no talk between the gunman and his hostages, and only slightly more between Peter and Mika as the day wore on. There were few questions about their situation they hadn't asked each other already, and most of those remained unanswered.

"Wahid," said Peter when the leader of the group delivered their supper that evening, "No one is coming. There are no stories, just like there is no rocket launcher. I am a freelance journalist with no employer, no wife, no family, no money I can get to and no life to leave behind. You must understand what this means for your plan."

Wahid's determination had begun to wane as the week drew to an end. He had been following the British news headlines, with one eye on his investment, while arguing with his family as he tried to justify the captivity, which was taking place in their home.

"And this Sarah?" asked Wahid.

"She's just a girl," said Peter, "We worked together. We had some laughs. We are good friends."

In the stark truth of being a hostage, he considered his lack of place in the world. His emphasising his own worthlessness to his captors had brought him little comfort. Even if he were to escape with his life, Peter didn't think it seemed like much of one to return to.

He would have found some solace in his peril if he felt he had more to lose: a family back home, a baby on the way, twenty years of service in the employment of a reputable company - these things would have increased his value and perhaps made him feel wanted. But he knew he was a keeper only for Sarah, and damn near worthless to everyone else.

He remembered her email.

and that also I think we are in love

and wanted to reply

...I think so a little bit, too.

In love. Peter assumed they were, or at least not alone in their solitude, which had deepened and run sweeter over the course of his captivity.

"She crosses my mind, you know?" he said to Wahid.

"And did you fuck her?" The question seemed vulgar, even to him, cold on the dark side of his loneliness.

"What do you want me to say, Wahid? I'm not going to lie to you. I did. I have nothing to gain in lying to you." Peter saw Wahid's remorse for his directness. He took a risk. "You have nothing to gain in keeping us. You know this."

Wahid looked to him for an explanation, inquisitive rather than accusatory. Peter pushed further. He thought no one would have replied to Wahid's demands. "You know no one will answer your emails."

Wahid held his silence. Peter kept talking.

"We can make another video, but no one will pay. NPL will not get the money you asked for to pay for the release of someone who doesn't work for them, but I'll bet you the same amount again that my colleagues will have tried. They would have gone to the head office in New York and it would have been flagged up to the United States government, who would then advise the British Foreign Office on its policy on journalists in hostage situations. I know that policy, Wahid. I was consulted on it.

"The kidnapping of a journalist will not be covered. Do you think that any reporter who visits Afghanistan would want to file a story about the high price his or her own capture would bring? It would only put their lives at risk.

"No one will publicise your demands. No one will chart our progress. There is no one to pay the ransom. We will either die here and the people who order the air strikes that will surely follow will have nothing to lose, or we can leave and they will have no reason to act. Your village in the valley is peaceful. You have a family and a house. You can let us go.

The British Army and US won't spend time chasing the wind. They can't even find the *real* enemy. You know this. You have a choice."

Wahid looked at Mika, who was staring at Peter.

"Wahid," said Peter, "this is the truth. The truth is all that matters."

And it will set us free, he thought.

Wahid stood. His face had softened and he looked beaten. The night fell with his spirit as he left the room.

36
Friday 27 August 2010
Gloucester Road

Sarah kicked off her shoes and poured herself some wine. The week she was hoping would end finally did, but another pursued it and she would be powerless to change her circumstances and weak to adapt to its challenges.

She drained half her glass and dialled a number on her home phone.

"Hello?"

"Hey Ma."

"Sarah, hon," said her mother. "How are you? Are you feeling better? *It's Sarah.*"

"Yeah, I guess. I was feeling low when I called you before. I didn't mean to jump down your throat."

"That's OK, sweetie. I know this must be hard for you with your missing friend."

Sarah didn't reply.

"Have you heard anything?" her mother asked.

"No," she said. She didn't mention the video. "We're still waiting for news."

"Is anyone out looking for him, this man?"

Sarah knew she had to stay guarded. In her exhaustion, she thought that her phone could be bugged, possibly by terrorists or the Foreign Office. She wondered if the police monitored the movements of wives and girlfriends of kidnap victims. None of this made sense, but she knew she couldn't discuss the particulars of the case. "I can't say too much about it, but there isn't much more I actually know."

"I'm so sorry for you. It can't be easy."

She felt herself starting to cry. "It's really not."

"Oh, baby," said her mother. Sarah sniffed. "This man - you obviously care for him a lot."

"More than he would ever let me," she said.

Sarah held the handset away from her face and she wiped her eyes with the bottom of her palm, the top of her hand clenched in a small fist. She returned the phone to her ear to catch her mother saying something quietly to her father.

"Sorry," said Sarah, "how have you guys been?"

"Us, we're just fine."

"How's Dad?"

"He's good. He's watching the hockey. Oh, did you see that game?"

"Which game?"

"I don't know, there was a game. The Devils? Is that the team he likes?"

"We don't really get the hockey out here."

The Devils were New Jersey's team, but her father was a Penguins fan. Being born in Harrisburg he had the choice as a boy between the Philadelphia Flyers and Pittsburgh Penguins, and he chose the team that had won the Stanley Cup the previous year.

"Just let me find out. Hang on." Her mother said something in the background. There was quiet and she called his name, "Ronny", and asked the questions. He replied patiently like he was telling her something for the first time, like the scheduled arrival time of a train.

Her mother came back on the phone. "The *Penguins.* I knew it began with a P."

Sarah coughed and chuckled. "I didn't see it, no."

"Sorry, honey, that would have bothered me," said her mother. "You'd think I'd know that. Isn't that awful? Penguins."

"It's all right," said Sarah. She was relieved to talk to her mother about something other than her own life.

"But yes, we're both well, don't worry, and have been thinking of you a lot."

"Thanks, Ma."

"If there's anything we can do, just let us know."

"I will," said Sarah.

"Or if you just want to pick up the phone, just go ahead. Day or night."

"I will. Thanks," said Sarah.

Her mother said goodbye half a dozen times in a variety of ways while Sarah continued to repeat her gratitude, which faded with each iteration, but remained heartfelt throughout her continued insistence before her mother finally hung up.

37
Friday 27 August 2010
Dubai

Jean Claude stepped out of the police car into the cool night and walked into the hallway of his apartment building.

He was looking forward to sleeping in his own bed after spending a night in a police cell. Agents Cohen and Jaworski had asked him questions about his connections with Al Qaeda and the Taliban and he had answered truthfully, but this didn't seem to satisfy the men from the CIA.

The local police chief didn't seem to mind the line of questioning, and Jean Claude guessed that following tenuous links to the terror networks was something that Dubai law enforcement tolerated on a regular basis.

Jean Claude was interviewed on the evening of his arrest, again on the following morning and was left alone with his thoughts in a small holding cell on Friday afternoon. That evening he repeated his story, which was as consistent as it was true.

"Yes," Jean Claude said, "I do have contacts with *links* to people close to Al Qaeda. These are the same informants you use."

"How do you know that, Mr. Charbonneau?" asked Randal Cohen.

"Look," said Jean Claude, "There aren't that many people in touch with both sides. I'm not able to give you the names of my contacts because it would put their lives in danger. It would also be bad for my stories and for your objectives."

Steven Jaworski stepped forward, stiffly in his wide suit. "These informants might be closer to the organisation than you are admitting," he said.

"Possibly, but they are not going to tell *me* where they sit within the organisation. Or you. If they say to me - 'Oh, Jean Claude, most of what I tell you is bullshit because I do not know what I am talking about because I am nobody and no one tells me anything' - why would I believe them ever again? Also, they are not going to say - 'By the way, I am second in command in Iraq'. This is not going to happen."

Jean Claude reached across the table to offer Agent Cohen a cigarette from a Marlboro box. Cohen refused with a frown.

Jean Claude continued. "They are sources. This is all. The information is right maybe half the time." He pronounced the l in half, as in shelf. "Maybe fifty, fifty five per cent. Sometimes half is good enough when there is nothing else."

The agents left the interrogation room and came back with the police chief who thanked Jean Claude for helping its American colleagues and told him an officer outside would drive him home.

Relieved to be back in his apartment, Jean Claude opened a beer and watched the news. He disagreed with the running order of the headlines Al Jazeera had chosen in his absence.

When the news finished he turned on his laptop and checked his email. Seeing there was nothing from Peter's Yahoo address or from Karl at NPL, he typed "Kabul" into Google and clicked on the map. His eye followed the A1 road, which ran from the capital to Kandahar, towards the southwest past Ghazni and Qara Bagh, both towns relatively quiet and peaceful places.

He knew Peter would have set off at midday and that Mika would have had more sense, even if his friend didn't, than to travel at night and the translator would have intended to make the seven-hour drive to Kandahar in a single trip.

If Mika had been running late, or if he had been delayed by a convoy or a security check, he would have stopped at a large town and found a room for the night, leading Jean Claude to assume they would have driven past Qalat. Any further on and they would have either been clear through to Kandahar, where it would be harder to carry out a kidnapping on a highway in the outskirts of the city. They wouldn't have pushed on beyond the Qalat after dark, and if they had reached Kandahar they would have checked into the hotel.

Looking at the map, he traced a line with his finger to along the A1 road to a point that was one-hour south west of Qalat. He followed the route to the bottom left of his screen, along the road further down across the sand-coloured terrain of the satellite image on the screen.

Jean Claude walked towards his bookshelf and took out a map of southern Afghanistan. There were three or four villages between Qalat and the Kandahar suburbs. One town stood out, set back from the road and isolated from the US military bases dotted along the highway.

It was called Meshdak, a small settlement - barely a town - more a collection of houses on a hillside and forty miles north east of Kandahar.

He dialled his office and spoke to the Duty Editor.

"Caleb," he said in English, "It's Jean Claude. Sorry it's late. Do we have a camera crew we use over the weekend for a job in Kandahar? It's important."

Jean Claude said he had a lead on Taliban activity near the Zabul province border just off the A1 to Kandahar. He explained away his arrest as being the result of misleading information and he had been cleared of any suspicion. He didn't mention the kidnapping of a journalist because he knew the camera crew would ask their colleagues if they knew who it was and it was important that Peter's disappearance remained a secret that couldn't spread to local correspondents, some of whom might have known Mika.

"There's a village they should go to called Meshdak. There are a few others in that region, but there are reports of Taliban activity and I think they should check out that one in particular, starting tomorrow. Double the rate for the weekend and short notice. We need a producer, camera operator, sound engineer and a reporter. There's no story at the moment and no brief because it's from a confidential source, but they should spend a couple of days in the area. I do not have many details, but there's something going on and we need to be on the ground. This is a big story and will run on the Arabic service."

Jean Claude knew this would help speed up the process. Footage for major events and breaking news were shared between the Arabic and English newsdesks. Caleb confirmed the details back. "Does it have to be tomorrow?" he said.

"Absolutely," said Jean Claude. "This is time critical."

The Duty Editor checked the rota and said the nearest local journalists on assignment were embedded at the Qalat Forward Operating Base, the US military station sixty miles away from Kandahar on the road to Kabul. "I can move them there tomorrow," he said.

"Thank you Caleb," said Jean Claude. "If they get any footage of local terrorist activity, we should put it on the air straight away. And anything involving foreign civilians or the military needs signoff by me."

Jean Claude said goodbye, finished his drink and went to bed.

38
Saturday 28 August 2010
Zabul Province

Peter noticed Samir had an expectant look when he brought them a breakfast of scrambled eggs and bread. Mika thanked him in Pashto and they started to eat. Peter noticed Samir was lingering in the room, holding the empty tray and wearing the shimmer of half a grin.

"Samir, what is it?"

"Peter, I can not say," he said. It was the first time Samir had used his name. Peter felt strangely validated.

"Samir, come on. How long have we known each other now? Six, seven days? What is it? It's the eggs, isn't it- is there something in the eggs?"

"No, no," said Samir, looking serious for a moment.

"Samir." They looked at each other. "Are we going home?"

Samir's eyes smiled. "Eat, please."

Mika and Peter watched him leave the room.

When they were alone, Mika spoke. "Today?" he asked, as if it were Peter's decision.

"It's going to be a morning, whenever it is," said Peter, buoyed by slight optimism. "They don't want us to die, as much for their sake as ours. Driving is too risky at night and they aren't going to come when we leave because they don't want to be seen with us.

We're a danger to them now. Our association with them is a threat."

"Perhaps we are worth something after all," said Mika.

"Thankfully not to them."

An hour after breakfast, Wahid entered with Zia, who looked surlier than ever. Wahid spoke before Peter could ask anything.

"You will leave tomorrow, with your car and your documents, on this condition."

"Go on," said Peter.

"You say this is a peaceful village. It must stay peaceful. I am not a terrorist. I am not a kidnapper and I will never repeat this -"

Peter looked at Zia, who looked mean and uninterested.

Wahid continued, "As we have nothing to gain by keeping you, you have nothing to gain in revenge."

Peter stood and said, "If you let us leave, we will continue our journey to Kandahar and we won't look for justice. Being delayed is not a crime."

Wahid pursed his lips in a concession of humility and Peter extended his hand.

"Tomorrow," said Wahid. He stepped forward and shook it, "We can't travel with you," he said.

"Thank you Wahid. I know you are a good man. You were thinking of your family."

"I meant you no harm."

"C'est la guerre," said Peter.

39
Sunday 29 August 2010
Zabul Province

In the seven days since their capture, the British and the American governments and armed forces had been unable to find the town where Peter Beckenham and Mika Hassan were being held. It took Al Qaeda less than forty-eight hours.

Zia was at the top of the organisation's list of local suspected kidnappers. He was a former young mujahideen from the war with the Russians. He had a military background and record for violent crime, had declined any offer to join the network. His refusal had annoyed the local Taliban commanders and his reputation as a tough character kept him on the fringes of Al Qaeda's attention.

He was known to them as a hired henchman for drug traffickers in the region. His age ruled him out as an active target for Al Qaeda recruiters, but its intelligence officers watched him in the hope that he could lead them to figures who might threaten its authority in the region, like opium drug lords or small time arms dealers who operated outside of the Taliban.

The terrorist organisation simply had to ring Peter's phone and wait for the call to divert to voicemail. No message was left, and Wahid, seeing that there were unanswered calls waiting, dialled in to check Peter's inbox. From there it was just a matter of

Al Qaeda using its contacts at the mobile network to determine the location of the incoming call which would lead them to the kidnappers.

The cellular information on the call revealed a coverage zone with a radius spanning twenty-five miles, an area which encompassed three villages.

The Commander was pleased with the news, and dispatched three local agents from the Kandahar area into Zabul province to hunt down the kidnappers and their captives. They travelled by day, under the cover of normal daily life, wearing local clothing, driving an old Toyota pickup truck like the ones used by the local farmers and traders.

The men carried out house-to-house inquiries in the villages and addressed crowds who assembled in the marketplaces. Some residents gathered out of fear, others from a sense of duty. The agents made sinister, weighted appeals for information from anyone who might know where the journalist and his companion were being held.

Would-be informants were promised rewards and glory, and the men threatened to punish anyone who withheld any knowledge relating to the kidnapping.

"We want to help," explained one of the terrorists to a group in a village marketplace. "As I speak to you now, the Americans are preparing to rescue these men and they will bomb your village to the ground. Whoever is holding these men is risking the lives of innocent people."

"We want peace in Afghanistan," said another

agent, "And every day while the blessed martyrs fight to protect their brothers from the infidels, these kidnappers in their greed will bring the invasion to your families."

They made their last appeal in Meshdak, a small village on the western slope of a valley along the road from Kabul to Kandahar. They studied faces in the assembled crowd, watching for signs of guilt or panic on certain cues in their address. They scanned the audience for a stir of interest at the opportunity of becoming an informant and obtaining a reward.

When the agents warned of the military threat, a young man in his early teens became increasingly concealed, hiding behind the dozen who had assembled by the well in the marketplace square. He crouched slightly behind a taller man, but remained in sight to hear what the men were saying. There was something about the boy, they thought.

One of the agents followed him as the crowd dispersed after the appeal and watched him speak to a man who drove him away in a silver BMW.

#

Peter took a breath of fresh air and felt the warmth of the sun on his back as it soothed the muscles, tightened by his final night's sleep on the couch.

He leaned over the back seat of the Honda to check again that he hadn't missed anything when he packed his bag. To his left he noticed a woman and a

small boy, no more than six years old, at the top of
the small staircase leading to the back door. She was
dressed in a smart, long embroidered scarlet dress and
wore a flowing headscarf that framed her face from
the forehead to the neckline.

Mika bowed his head to the woman, who nodded
once as a response in a guarded respect. They stood
in the clear, free morning, looking forward to their
lives resuming while the hope seeped in. Peter
straightened his back and the boy waved at him. He
returned the greeting with a smile. The mother tapped
her son without emotion and he went back into the
house. Peter put his hand to his heart to display his
gratitude, and the woman turned in an ebb of sequins
and disappeared inside.

Samir emerged from the front of the house,
smiling as he approached. Peter saw he was holding
something carefully in a small towel.

"Please, no more eggs, ok, Samir?" said Peter, half
smiling.

Samir looked over his shoulder and walked past
Peter to the far side of the Honda. Peter followed and
Samir stepped to stand close to him. He unwrapped
the item gingerly and spoke in a quiet tone. "You will
take it."

Wahid's pistol sat in the folds of the fabric, held by
Samir like an offering.

"Samir...," Peter pleaded softly in kindness, "What
the fuck am I supposed to do with this?"

"Please, take it," said Samir.

"I can't steal from you. Besides, how am I going to use it? Even if I'd had one when you picked me up, I wouldn't have pulled a gun on you. It probably would have got me killed. I can't take it, I'm sorry, but god bless you, man." He shook his head in affectionate disbelief.

Samir was warmed by the sentiment of the refusal, which seemed kinder in the glow of Peter's chuckle at the irony of an atheist blessing his kidnapper for offering him a stolen gun.

Samir wrapped the pistol and held the package at his side, unsure what to say next.

"There is one thing," said Peter.

"Yes," said Samir, almost relieved at the prospect of being of service.

"Our phones need charging."

Samir went back in the house to investigate and Peter started packing his small travel bag.

Wahid denied the request to charge the phones. He did not want them to be used within range of the house in case Peter and Mika called for help and revealed their location to the British or American armies. He gave Peter his BlackBerry and Mika his Nokia without the chargers and with the batteries run down.

After packing his bag, Peter showered and helped Mika finish loading the car. Zia pulled up in the BMW with Ali in the passenger seat. He brought the car to a sudden stop and walked quickly inside the house, not even stopping to look at his former captives. Peter heard him talking to Wahid, who came outside two minutes later.

Wahid spoke quickly and quietly. "Three men in the village have been asking about a kidnapping. Zia said Ali heard them talking about an English journalist. They were dressed in traditional clothing of the mujahideen"

Zia and Samir were inside, talking quickly, exchanging information and responding with varying degrees of consent.

"What does that mean?" Peter pictured the earth-coloured robes and the pakol hats worn by the Taliban, but he didn't understand the significance of their presence in the village.

"These men are Al Qaeda. They will kill you," said Wahid.

"They'll kill *you*," said Peter, "How did they-"

Samir came out of the house and approached them, carrying his AK47. "Peter. There is no time. You must hide. Inside. Please."

"No," said Peter.

Wahid looked puzzled.

"Peter, we must," said Mika.

"Wahid," said Peter, emoting with skyward palms, "if we go in your house and these men find us we will all die. If we leave now, we have a chance to get away and you might live."

Wahid turned to Samir, who offered no reply, then looked back at Peter with a mixture of determination and resignation.

"We have to go. *Now*," said Peter.

"OK," said Wahid. Peter and Mika got into the car and closed the doors. They shook Wahid's hand through the open window. Zia appeared at the doorway to watch them leave, with Ali standing behind, wide-eyed, though he managed to smile at Peter.

"Take the road to the left," said Wahid. "You must not go on the road you took to come here. If they come it will be from Meshdak."

"It was dark when we got here. All I know is we went up a hill when we left the road," said Peter. "Meshdak?"

"The village below," said Wahid, pointing down into the valley. He looked at Mika and gave him directions in Pashto.

Samir translated for Peter's sake. "After the gate, go left. You will avoid the village. Three kilometres, then west."

Peter spoke, deliberately to Samir. "Thank you." Samir looked at him and brought his hands together to hold them as a display of sincerity. Peter's voice warbled with gratitude and fear. "Go inside. Have lunch. Go to work. Hide the guns. Watch a movie. Be safe."

He looked to Mika who started the engine on his cue. Peter nodded in appreciation to Wahid.

"Go with god," said Wahid.

"Insha'Allah," said Peter. Mika smiled at his accent.

Peter pointed a finger back and forth from Wahid to Samir in mock resolute admonishment. "And *no more* kidnapping."

Samir smiled and they both stepped back as Mika drove them away.

Mika followed Wahid's instructions and took the road that led them away from the village, wound further into the hills and headed away from the highway that ran from Kabul to Kandahar. They weren't sure where it would lead, but they were certain that putting distance between them and Meshdak was safer than driving towards the Al Qaeda agents.

They drove into the end of the clear afternoon. Peter looked at the sun and said, "We're sort of heading west. West-southwest, which is kind of towards Kandahar."

Mika remained quiet, concentrating on the road surface and checking the rearview mirror for signs of anyone following them.

"With some luck we'll get to the highway," Peter continued, "but in the meantime at least we've got some miles between us and -" he paused.

"-Meshdak."

"*Mesh*dak," Peter said, impatient with his forgetful nature. He leaned over to Mika and looked at the fuel gauge. "We've got what, half a tank?"

"Just over, yes."

"That won't get us back to Kabul. We're out of the area where we were kidnapped, but we can't keep going because we don't want to be driving at night. We'll need to stop in the next hour or so."

"Where?"

"Anywhere we won't be seen from the road," said Peter. "We can get going again in the morning. Does that sound good?"

"It sounds better than Jimmy Nelson," said Mika.

"OK, for a start, it's *Willie* Nelson," said Peter. "All right? And second, when we get back? You and me are going to have a little sit down. There's nothing wrong with a bit of Willie Nelson. That's music from the heart. That's the stuff of life, right there. You just lack the proper foundations."

"I see," said Mika, humouring him.

"You need a little groundwork. A little TLC. I'm talking Tammy, Lovett, Cash. Country music will tear your heart and mend your soul. And I haven't played any Willie Nelson so far today, but you keep pushing and we may need an intervention."

Mika smiled and looked ahead.

"Jimmy *Nelson*," said Peter quietly.

As dusk approached they pulled off the hard dirt road into a depression, a clearing among the small hills that hid them from any passing traffic, although the road seemed deserted.

They piled on layers of clothing, tilted the front seats back into makeshift recliners and waited for sleep to find them.

Mika looked out the window into the failing light. The sky was breaking out in stars, and each one of the millions stood proud and alone in a backdrop to the moon.

"We will have to find a route south soon. I believe that's the direction to the A1 which leads to Kandahar," Mika said.

Peter folded a t-shirt into a square to fashion a crude pillow, and placed it under his head. "You think perhaps we should ask someone?" he said.

Mika laughed and Peter joined in so much the car shook, and the noise filled their souls.

Peter waited until the joy faded. "Hey Mika?"

"Yes."

"Thanks."

"It's OK."

"No. Thanks." Peter rolled his shoulder against the backrest. "And I'm sorry, but thank you."

Mika's tone was gracious and accepting. "You're welcome."

Peter took a deep breath, deep and loud, as if willing on the sleep.

Mika added: "We're not home yet, though."

Peter lifted his head. "Why do you have to go and spoil everything?" he joked. "We were having a laugh, a heartfelt moment and you come up with the negative."

"Good night, Peter," said Mika, with comedy impatience.

"*Jeez.* I should have accepted the gun from Samir when I had the chance."

"Good *night,* Peter."

"If you say so."

They laughed a little more, and fell into a hard, free sleep.

40
Monday 30 August 2010
Hammersmith

Sarah stood in her kitchen as 9am drifted past. She scanned through the messages on her phone for a sign from Peter. She decided to eat something, if only to take her mind of the lack of communication from him. She ate a piece of toast with studied mouthfuls, as if rehearsing the activity of chewing, but her mind drifted back to him every time she realised she was not remembering. She hoped he missed her too, and that it brought comfort in his loneliness. She thought of him as a solitary figure, not just in captivity but in the world he had landscaped for himself, which she imagined was a wonderful and solitary place. She wondered if the longer he were missing, the more he would feel that she was all he had. She winced at the selfishness of the thought and forced down another mouthful.

On the newsdesk, Jim was sifting through the morning stories ahead of his regular ten o'clock meeting with the Homepage editor and colleagues from the Entertainment and Business desks who would be briefed by whoever had worked the early News shift. Together they would run through the agenda before picking the leads that Jim would share across the department.

"Jeez," Jim said to Carla.
"What is it?"

"This story here on the Al Jazeera site: 'A boy has been killed by suspected Al Qaeda agents in the village of Meshdak in the Zabul province of Afghanistan. After an exchange of gunfire, Ali Niazi, thirteen, was taken from his house in front of his parents at midday on Sunday 29 August before being shot and killed in the village marketplace."

"God, that's awful."

Jim kept reading. "'A spokesman for the Afghan police said the area was generally regarded as safe and free of Al Qaeda or Taliban activity and it would be reassessing its operations while working closely with the British and US security forces in that area. The boy's family were taken into custody for their own safety.'"

"That's shocking," said Carla.

"There's a video as well," said Jim.

"Are you thinking of running it?"

"We'd never get approval. Besides, would you want to watch it?"

"Probably not," she said.

"Exactly," he said.

"Should we lead with it as a text story?"

"No," said Jim, "it won't get the numbers. This happens all the time. Stick it in the Alsos."

"OK."

Carla logged into the content management system and started to edit the page.

"Coffee?" asked Jim.

Carla smiled. "I will, thank you."

41
Monday 30 August 2010
Near the border of the Zabul and Kandahar provinces

Dawn crept into the clearing, and the early sun filtered through the condensation on the windscreen. Stretched out as horizontal as he could manage, Peter opened his eyes and looked at the pale sky. He turned to find himself alone in the car and a knot tightened inside him.

He wondered whether to keep his head down while he listened for sounds of Mika, or others. He looked at the mirrors but from the angle of his semi-reclined position under the window he could only see the roof of the passenger compartment and the slope of a distant hill.

He grew tense as he shuffled his stiff body forward until he was crouched in the foot well of the passenger side, where he waited.

Silence. No pad of footsteps or crumple of tyres across the dirt. He raised his eyes to the bottom of the passenger side window, but saw only peaks rising from the clearing where they had spent the night. He lifted his head higher to see the tops of scrubby bushes and weeds shifting in the dry wind. He rose up more but there was still no sign of Mika. He expected to turn to see him beyond the far side of the car, on his knees with his hands behind his head and a figure at his back - Zia with his shotgun. He imagined the echo the thud of a shotgun would make as the shot reported off the soft hills, but he saw nothing other than the landscape. He turned to look out the driver's side window and saw Mika twenty feet away, on his knees, bent at the waist and not moving, crumpled and face down on the ground. Peter's heart rang in his ears and he thought he was going to vomit as he looked at his friend's still body on the dirt. His eyes darted to the back window as he looked for a gunman, but he saw no one.

Mika moved - barely noticeably at first - it was a small shuffle which grew more deliberate as he unravelled himself and sat up on his haunches, uttering something, before returning to the ground in a deep, humble bow.

"Oh for fuck's sake," said Peter out loud to himself in relief.

He hoisted himself climbed back into his seat and stretched out the tension of anxiety and sore muscles before opening the door.

He walked towards Mika stiffly. "You're praying," he said.

Mika finished a solemn phrase and turned his quiet focus onto Peter. "Yes," he said.

He sounded calm, almost proud.

"You never prayed before."

Mika shrugged as he rose from his knees. "No."

Peter stood next to him. "Guess it felt like a praying moment," he said. He scanned the horizon. The hills rose smallest directly in front of them. "Any idea where we are?"

Mika patted himself down. "We must find a way south, then west," he said.

Peter looked ahead to the morning sun, then at the tracks that peeled away behind the car. "We've been driving through a valley," he said, "I don't know, but we need to get back on highway. We can either go back the way we came or we can keep going. If they *are* Al Qaeda we want as much space as possible between them and us, and hope they don't find Wahid."

They left the clearing and carried on their route. The dirt road turned towards the south, where small towns clung to ever steeper hillsides. They were hungry, but Peter craved a phone battery more than breakfast. He wanted to contact Sarah and tell her he was all right, and free, and to find out if she was too.

The track led them through the foothills, where the surface turned to paved road and they drove through the cool morning. The hills faded to flat land as the horizon bristled with buildings on the outskirts of the town, breaking the dull surface of the earth as Mika drove them towards Kandahar.

They pulled off the road at a small restaurant just inside the city boundary and sat down at one of the bare tables. There were two men at the counter of a bar, breaking off their argument to look at Mika and Peter between their declarations.

"How do you feel about this place?" asked Peter, glancing at the men.

"They are arguing about wheat prices," said Mika.

Peter avoided eye contact with the owner when he brought him a plate of palao, a rice dish. Peter nodded a brief thank you to acknowledge its arrival.

"Should we ask to use their phone?" asked Mika.

"I don't know. The owner could check the last number dialled, and it could identify us. This may not be the best fitting expression out here, but we're not out of the woods yet. Maybe he could charge our phones."

Mika considered this briefly. "I don't think it would be good if people called us here, or if the phones left our sight."

"I guess not," said Peter. "Also, if we start up our phones it will identify where we are. Who knows where that might lead."

Peter amused himself with the idea of troops swinging into action in response to his mobile phone signal coming back online. It seemed absurd, but he didn't want to take any risks in a situation already so far beyond his area of expertise.

Afghanistan? Karl and Sarah had both asked. *And as it turned out*, Peter thought, *they had a point*.

"No," he said, "let's just get to the hotel. How far to go now?"

"About twenty minutes," said Mika.

The owner took the money for the food and sold them some petrol that he poured out of a jerry can into their tank.

Peter and Mika drove to the Armani Hotel where

they had been expected eleven days earlier. There was a small lobby area with a half dozen armchairs next to an unattended bar. A television was on but no one was watching it. Some men sat by a magazine stand near the staircase.

The man at reception explained that their reservation had been held open for them at the expense of a Mr. Howard in London. He handed Peter a piece of paper.

Date: 26 August 2010. 16:29:37 GMT+1
From: Karl.Howard@corp.npl.com
To: ArmaniHotel@neda.af
Subject: Welcome home
Message:

Welcome home, mate. Be in touch when you get this mail.

Karl.

The receptionist told Peter there were two American men waiting for him in his room.

"A welcoming committee from Uncle Sam," Peter said quietly to Mika. He noticed three large western-looking men in their early twenties sitting at the entrance to the stairway. They looked like US Marines, thick-necked and disciplined, wearing civilian clothing.

Peter asked to use a phone. He wasn't sure how much privacy he would have in his room and he wanted to call Karl. As he dialed, a dramatic graphics sequence on the television signaled the start of a news bulletin. Mika walked towards it as the headlines started.

Peter reached Karl's voicemail. It was 10am in Kandahar and 7:30am in the UK and his former boss wouldn't be in the office yet. Peter noticed Mika gravitating toward the grainy images of the newscast in a slow pull while the voicemail greeting message played. There was footage of grieving and energetic movement in the bloody rust red dusk. Mika stiffened, chilled.

BEEP

"Karl. It's Peter. It's Monday morning, 30 August and I'm in Kandahar. I got your message, I'm free, and I'm safe."

He reeled off these facts like items on a shopping list, dulling down the tone to the mundane to provide reassurance.

"I'll call back, OK? I'm in the hotel with Mika Hassan and I'm in the reception and I can't really say any more than that, but I'm all right. *We're* all right. I got your email. Thanks mate. Look, I'll talk to you later. Cheers."

He hung up and joined Mika in front of the television, which showed pictures of US armoured personnel carriers next to two British Land Rovers.

"Who's winning?" asked Peter.

Mika eyes stayed fixed on the screen. "This is Meshdak."

"*Our* Meshdak?" said Peter.

"They are saying the Americans have arrested a family."

"No."

Mika didn't reply.

"Wahid?" said Peter.

"They say a child was killed in the village. He was from the same family."

Peter steadied himself, and Mika said it. "I think this is the boy."

"Ali," said Peter.

A small arm briefly occupied the corner of a frame filled with wails and confusion, an image which failed to capture anything more detailed than suffering.

Peter stood rooted in shock next to Mika.

"Jesus," said Peter, "I just... this day needs to fucking end."

Mika turned his head to listen to the commentary and the item ended and the shot returned to the presenter in the studio who wore a grave expression and introduced a segment that started with a shot of a government building.

"What else did they say?" asked Peter.

Mika answered just as quietly. "They said it looked like a public execution. They said the family was at home, there was a gun battle, and he was taken. The family is now with the Americans."

"They would have had to take them into custody," said Peter. "Ali was killed to punish them for kidnapping us. They found Wahid's family because they we looking for us."

"Who?" Mika considered his words. "The Network?"

"Don't say it," said Peter, looking around with a calmness at odds with his quick instruction. "There are some Americans in my room. Do you want to join me?"

Mika nodded.

"You sure? It's up to you."

Mika sniffed, resolute. "Yes," he said.

#

US authorities were informed of all murders in Afghanistan, which bore the hallmark of Al Qaeda executions. After Ali's death, the Americans placed his grieving family under arrest not only for their own protection but also to question them about any information about the terrorist network.

Wahid has been shot in the leg in the brief exchange of gunfire that took place when Ali was taken. He was treated in hospital where he explained to the CIA that he had abducted Peter Beckenham and Mika Hassan for the ransom money, and that he didn't know anything about any Al Qaeda agents until they turned up in Meshdak, and that he had never had any links to the group until they murdered his only son.

Zia said very little, which aroused the suspicion of the US authorities, and Samir told them everything he knew, and asked if Peter and Mika had made it to safety.

Despite all three stories matching, the CIA thought the three men might be linked to terrorists, and Wahid found himself making a case for his own unimportance, arguing that his detention would not worry any real members of Al Qaeda, and neither sleeper cells in Kandahar nor the Taliban mujahideen cared whether he lived or died, as his injury had proven.

#

Peter and Mika carried their bags past the three men sitting by the stairway and carried their bags up the flight of stairs and walked down the hallway. A solidly built American man with large shoulders was standing at the far end of the corridor outside what Peter presumed to be his room.

"It's this way," said Peter to Mika as they approached the doorway behind the man.

"I'm Peter Beckenham," he said to the man who stood as if to challenge everyone who might be listening. "This is my room. Step aside."

Peter enjoyed being rude to the man, who would have snapped someone like a twig if they had spoken to him like that in the Silk Road bar. Peter understood the man was there on official business, and that his job was to prevent trouble from happening instead of causing it. The man knocked on the door and Peter moved around him, put his key in the lock and entered the room. A man in a dark suit stood up from his seated position on the bed and stepped towards the door. A taller man, also smartly dressed, was in a chair at the small desk to the far end of the room by its large and only window.

"Mr. Beckenham?" said the standing man.

"Yes?"

"I'm Agent Randal Cohen, this is Agent Steven Jaworski from the United States Central Intelligence Agency. We'd like to ask you a few questions."

"So would I. Namely: where the fuck have you been and why are you in my room?"

Agent Jaworski stood. "Mr. Beckenham," he said, "Agent Cohen and I are conducting a counter-terrorism investigation. We know you've been through a lot with your abduction."

"I'm not surprised you know about that, but I'd be interesting in knowing how you do."

Agent Cohen spoke. "Wahid Niazi and his family are in the protective custody of the United States. Mr. Niazi and his accomplices have been questioned about their connection to Al Qaeda and we'd like to talk to you and Mr. Hassan about your perception of their involvement."

"You've arrested them?"

"This is an ongoing investigation in the war on terror," Agent Jaworski answered.

"They kidnapped me for money. I'm certain that they were acting alone, under Wahid's direction.

Somehow, and I don't know how it happened, Al Qaeda found out about it and came after them. I would imagine they don't take kindly to private kidnappings. That's it," said Peter, "that's where his involvement ends."

"Mr. Beckenham, wake up," said Agent Cohen. "Wahid Niazi kidnapped you and demanded money from your former employer, NPL. When that failed he changed his plan, intending to hand you over to hostile forces in that area on the day you and Mr. Hassan escaped."

"We didn't escape - we shook their hands and drove away. Wahid was going to release us anyway because he knew he wasn't going to get his ransom. One of them tried to give me a gun. They are not killers. If anything, our release was brought forward because they discovered Al Qaeda had found out we'd been kidnapped by people outside of the organisation."

Peter looked at Mika, then back to the men. "They knew they had to get us out before we were discovered in their custody," he said. "We had become a threat to *their* safety. My guess is that Al Qaeda found out about us because half the world's press knew we had been taken. I'm guessing the media didn't report it because they didn't want to raise our value - something small time kidnappers didn't have the experience or reputation to do on their own."

Agent Cohen shook his head. "Mr. Beckenham,

you're too naive."

Peter raised his voice. "Now listen," he said, "you have no grounds to detain that family unless it's for their own safety."

"Mr. Niazi is a potential threat to national security," said Agent Jaworski. "He's an injured enemy combatant."

"Injured?" asked Peter.

"He was shot in the leg during a firefight at the scene of the abduction," said Agent Cohen. "It happened before we were able to apprehend them."

"Is he all right?" asked Peter.

Agent Cohen looked at his colleague and back to Peter. "He'll be fine," he said, "he'll remain in our custody. End of story."

"There'll be a real story if you *don't* release Wahid," said Peter. He motioned rapidly between himself and Mika. "Son of a diplomat and a digital journalist - you think people won't listen to us?"

"*Ex* digital journalist," said Agent Cohen.

"You think I can't influence the fucking agenda, college boy? The world's media wouldn't report my *kidnapping* out of respect for me. Some *ex*. Let's see how the world likes a CIA blunder in a war zone, and how they tore apart a family they couldn't convict because there was no evidence and the victim dropped the charges?" he said. "There. I've dropped the charges. Over. Done."

"This isn't disturbing the peace, son," said Agent Cohen. Peter moved further into the room while

Mika stayed by the bathroom door at the entrance, with their bags at his feet.

"This isn't *terrorism*!" shouted Peter. "If you hold these people, I promise you there will be 'Free Wahid' websites from here to eBay."

"They had weapons," said Agent Jaworski.

"They needed weapons! Where do you think we are? Their son was killed in the fucking street!"

"Because they were kidnappers," said Agent Cohen.

"And is that justice?" asked Peter. "Killing the children of kidnappers? And then you let the killers go free?"

"That's an internal matter for the Afghan authorities," said Agent Jaworski. "This became a diplomatic issue when they kidnapped a foreign journalist and the son of an Egyptian minister."

"So our lives matter more because of selective racism, is that right? This story is shaping up already. Mika, can we set up some video here really quickly?"

Mika stared back blankly, unsure if Peter was serious.

"I'm sorry you see it this way," said Agent Cohen.

"There's no other way to see it," Peter replied. "But no, really, why don't you tell your side of the story? Let's get some mics on you and Captain America here."

The men looked at each other and moved past Peter towards the door.

"Mika, get a white balance reading and I'll start

looking at high impact blog templates and web site names."

Mika stepped aside to clear the exit for the men while Peter paced and brainstormed ideas out loud and production plans involving mailing lists, website forums and publishing platforms.

"*Free Wahid*" said Peter, in an aspirational tone as he faced the window and looked out into middle distance, his heart beating faster. He made the span of an imaginary headline in his hands.

The agents stepped around Mika.

"One second," said Peter, "let me check the audio levels."

He wrenched a desk lamp from its socket and threw it against the wall above the bed's headboard. It shattered, spraying the room with porcelain fragments. The agents stood by the bathroom, staring at Peter while he considered the room's acoustics.

"It's been a long week," Mika explained. The men walked out and he closed the door behind them. He turned and stared at Peter in shock but not disbelief.

Peter, breathing heavily, said, "Um. Sorry about the lamp. They had to think I was irrational."

"I could have told them that."

Peter smiled. Mika pointed at himself. "Character witness," he said.

Mika chuckled and walked towards Peter, stepping around pieces of broken pottery. Peter sat on the end of the bed, laughing - tentatively at first, then forcefully, his shoulders shaking as he leant forward with his elbows on his knees.

Mika sat next to him, his own laugh reduced to a series of exhalations. Peter's head went down into his hands as the cackles turned into silent convulsing, then sobbing and long mournful moans and sniffs. He leaned into Mika, who held his friend's shaking, sorry frame as he wept.

42
Monday 30 August 2010
Gloucester Road

Sarah left her flat half way through the morning and in no hurry. She locked the door of her flat and was walking towards the tube station when her phone signaled the arrival of a text message.

Peter Beckenham

She clicked on his name.

Do you know how hard it is to buy a charger for a BlackBerry in Kandahar?

Sarah's thumb fumbled and scrolled for his number. He answered.

"Kandahar."

"Oh god, it's you." Her voice broke.

"Hey, baby."

"Oh god..." Sarah started to cry, suddenly in a gust of sadness. "Peter." Her voice was a collusion of sweet anger and relief. "Peter - oh god, the times I thought I'd lost you."

"I know," he said. "Me too."

"It's so good to talk to you."

"I'm sorry. You know I would have called earlier."

"What happened? How are you?"

"Oh so *now* you want a story."

"Shut up, Peter," she said. "Please..."

"They let me go. They weren't such bad guys after all, and some even worse guys came after them. Or me. But they let us go. And I'm all right."

"Oh Jesus. I was so worried. I can't tell you - thank you. Thank you for calling me."

"You're the first person I've spoken to. I left a message with Karl earlier. Tell him I'm OK. Are you on your way to work?"

"Yes. And I will. And also?" she said.

"What?"

"You called me 'baby'."

"When? No I didn't," said Peter.

She laughed, holding back the emotion. "Just now you did."

"Whatever. You keep thinking that."

"I love you."

"So I *hear*," he said self-consciously, "I got your email. I've been meaning to reply. You know how it is."

There was a pause between them. "They mailed me," she said.

"I thought they might have," said Peter. "I'm sorry. It wasn't as bad as it looked."

"That's good." She struggled to say the words in a small voice.

Peter tried to raise the mood. "So how much were they asking for?"

"Ten million."

"*Pounds?*"

"Dollars."

"That's *it*? And New York wouldn't cough up?"

"You're not an employee," said Sarah. "It's policy more than principle."

"I know. And you don't negotiate with terrorists."

"Apparently not," she said.

Peter coughed. "Look, I'll let you go. Tell Karl or Jim to call me. I'm presuming Jim knows about the kidnapping."

"You have no idea, do you?"

"Very little, in fact. I had the CIA in my hotel room yesterday. Cunts, as it turns out."

Sarah laughed. A sigh, then, "So what now?"

"What, what now?"

"I mean what now."

"You mean, with *us* what now?"

"Mmmm."

"Well, I'm leaving Afghanistan, I know that much. I don't know how these things work, there may be some kind of debrief or something. I guess I'll be back there in a few days."

"I could take time off." She raised her voice in a tentative hope at the end of the sentence.

"You could take what off?" he said.

"Stop it."

"What? It's a really bad line," he said.

Sarah was worried about how his ordeal might have affected the man she knew she loved.

"Are you OK?" she asked.

"Yeah. I need to get back to Kabul and I assume

there'll be some kind of operation to get me home. I guess I'll be *extracted*," He thought about that term. "Ew. - No, I'm fine, honest."

"No, I mean are you *OK*? Do you feel, I don't know - changed?"

"People don't change. Look, we've been over this. Life changes, people *adapt*."

"I know..." she said.

"But I am, thanks. Our lives have changed and we'll adapt to them," he said. "If you want to."

"I want to."

"Good. Why? Wait - have *you* changed?

"No."

"Then I still love you," he said.

She was caught off guard by his honesty. Thrown, but hopeful. "Don't be home too late," she said.

"You're sounding like a girlfriend already."

"Is that OK now?"

"I don't know, I've just spent a week as a hostage. I *guess* I could get used to it."

"You're funny," she said.

They each stood in their respective worlds, both in harmony and time in the place where Peter's head caught up with his heart.

"Have a good day at work," he said.

"I will," she answered.

"Bye honey."

ABOUT THE AUTHOR

Cliff Jones works in digital media, tweets regularly as @Cliff, and lives in Berkshire in the UK.

Water Runs Slow Through Flat Land is a work of fiction. Any resemblance between characters in the book and real life people is coincidental, apart from William Hague.

Printed in Great Britain
by Amazon